The Blue Wings

The Blue Wings

JEF AERTS

Illustrated by Martijn van der Linden

Translated by Laura Watkinson

Montclair | Amsterdam | New York

This is an Em Querido book

Published by Levine Querido

www.levinequerido.com • info@levinequerido.com

Levine Querido is distributed by Chronicle Books LLC

Library of Congress Control Number 2019953556

ISBN 978-1-64614-008-4

Printed and bound in China.

Published September 2020

First Printing

For all giants, big or small

Sprig

IT WAS THE FIRST DAY of fall break and all we had planned was lots of fun stuff together. Like watching cranes, for example.

My brother Jadran and I raced each other along the path through the woods to the lake. He ran ahead of me in his rubber boots. I let him win. Everyone let Jadran win. Even though he was as strong as a young wolf, his big, gangling body was slow.

And he couldn't stand losing.

"Watch out, Giant, I'm catching up with you!" I shouted to fire him up.

And Jadran liked being fired up. He staggered across the stones to the squelchy shore. As usual, his head hung slightly forward and his back was hunched.

"I want to be the first to see them," he panted. "I'm always the first to see everything, aren't I, Josh?"

The sound of trumpeting came from behind the reeds.

Krrroo krrroo krrroo!

Jadran turned and waved at Mom and Murad, who were strolling to the lake, arm in arm. Yasmin trudged along behind them, doing her best not to see any cranes at all. She'd wrapped her scarf high over her face, right up to her glasses.

"I can already hear them!" shouted Jadran. "That counts too, doesn't it, Mom?"

Mom and Murad gave a thumbs up, both at the same time. And that made them both laugh, also at exactly the same moment.

Murad and his daughter had only just moved into our apartment last week. And it hadn't exactly gone smoothly. It had taken forever before Jadran would say a word to Murad. The night of the move he had barricaded the front door with a dresser. The only thing that eventually saved the situation was the promise that he could sleep in my room from now on, on two mattresses pushed close together.

Jadran ran clumsily toward the sound of the cranes, his chin sticking out and his big hands dangling beside his body.

"Josh, make sure he doesn't go too far!" Mom screamed above the wind. "He's not allowed near the marsh!"

I sprinted after him. Jadran was sixteen and could lift me up in the air with one arm. But even though he was almost five years older than me, he was my little brother as far as Mom was concerned.

We squelched our way over to a bed of reeds, Jadran squawking along with the cranes. With every step, his feet sank deeper into the mud.

Krrroo krrroo krrroo.

We saw the huge birds among the reeds, pecking for food. There were dozens of them, with their long legs and their bushy tail feathers. They had patches of red on their heads, and their black-and-white necks jerked back and forth.

"There they are!" shrieked Jadran, way too loud. He threw his arms in the air and made a leap toward the birds. The cold water splashed and soon he was up to his calves in the sludge.

"Shut up, Giant," I whispered, but it was already too late. They'd spotted us. The crane alarm went off.

Kaa kroo-ee! Kaa kroo-ee!

The birds turned to stone, heads forward, high on their toes. Only their beaks still moved, making that eerie cry.

"You scared them," I hissed.

"But I didn't do anything, did I?" Jadran plowed on through the reeds. "Don't be scared, my friends. I'm coming to see you!"

"Jadran, stop there!" Mom called from the shore.

That basically meant: *Stop him, Josh!*

I slid my sleeves over my hands so I wouldn't cut myself on the sharp leaves. My brother thrashed wildly with his arms and crushed the reeds under his feet. The cranes spread their wings and cried louder and louder.

Kaa kroo-ee! Kaa kroo-ee!

"Just wait, Giant!" I shouted.

Jadran cupped his hands around his mouth and yelled, "I'm not going to hurt you! I never hurt anyone!"

And then, all at once, they took off.

It was pandemonium, a thundercloud of feathers. The cranes bumped into one another, skimmed past the pine trees, and flapped away as fast as they could.

Startled, Jadran took a step back and sank knee-deep into the mud.

"Stay calm," I said soothingly. "Take a deep breath."

Mom and Murad hurried toward us along the lake path. Yasmin had grabbed her phone and started filming everything, just for fun.

"They have to stay here!" shouted Jadran.

"Never mind," I said. "They'll be back soon."

Jadran splashed the water with the palms of his hands. "They're flying away, aren't they? In the winter they live in Spain—that's what you said!" The duckweed sloshed up onto his butt.

The cranes gathered and glided in two low lines across the water. You could hear the swish of their feathers as they flapped their wings. I took Jadran's hand and dragged him out of the slurping mud before his boots got completely stuck.

"Look, they want to say goodbye," I said, steering Jadran back to solid ground. "Cranes make letters in the sky—did you know that?"

Jadran shook his head. But he still looked back at the birds, which were flying higher and higher.

"*U*!" he shouted.

"So they can talk to each other, all the way from Finland to the Mediterranean Sea," I said.

Jadran nodded and started pointing here and there. "And look, that wobbly line over there, that's an *S*!"

I led Jadran to the wooden jetty, which was packed with boats in the summertime. Yasmin was standing on the edge, filming herself with the flying cranes.

"Here, here, here!" said Jadran, trying to lure them back.

Krrroo krrroo krrroo-ee!

"Hey, they're calling to me, aren't they?"

Yasmin indignantly stopped filming. "Don't be so dumb."

"Jadran is not dumb!" I said.

He squeezed my hand tighter and tighter. "It's my fault."

"Shh," I said.

"Everything's always my fault, isn't it?"

His arm was shaking. My fingers were cracking.

"Not everything, Giant."

"How much?"

"No more than half."

THE CRANES DID A FINAL spin around the lake and then disappeared among the wispy clouds. An airplane drew a line through their letters.

Jadran's pant legs were dripping, and his face was covered in splashes of mud. The duckweed was up to my knees.

"Look at the state of you two!" said Murad, and it almost sounded like a compliment. As always, he was wearing shiny shoes and pants with an ironed crease down the front.

Mom took a tissue from her bag and began to clean Jadran's cheeks. He stood there like a little kid, even though he was a head-and-a-half taller than her.

"Next time stay close to us," she said. "And don't go running off into the water."

Ee-oo! came a sudden cry from some nearby trees. Jadran pushed Mom's hand away. The tissue fell to the ground and blew off into the reeds.

"What's that?" he said.

Ee ee ee-oo!

Yasmin was the first to follow the squeaking sounds. She lifted her feet carefully so that her sneakers didn't get dirty. And of course we weren't going to let her go on her own.

Mom shouted, "I just told you to stay close to us, Giant!"

But we were already dashing off.

The shrill cries were coming from under a hazel bush. I pushed the branches aside so that we could get closer. Among the leaves, there was a tall, thin bird. It was a young crane, with its beak open wide. Its feathers were still brownish, and its neck wasn't the same beautiful black-with-a-white-stripe that the older birds had.

"He's panicking," I whispered.

Jadran was shaking with excitement, and he clenched his hands. "They've forgotten him!"

"Look," said Yasmin. "He can't leave."

I crouched beside the young bird. He kicked out, but couldn't reach me. His wing was tangled in a piece of fishing line.

"He's bleeding!" shouted Jadran.

"Poor thing," said Yasmin.

Murad came to help us. He showed me how to stop

the bird from moving. Holding the bird's legs tight with one hand, he untangled the fishing line with the other. The down under the bird's left wing was matted with blood.

"He's gotten the hook stuck in him," said Murad.

I slid my fingers under the wing and lifted it so that Murad could pull the fishhook out of the wound. Quick as a flash, the bird pecked me.

"Ow!" Yasmin jumped back as if it was *her* hand he'd jabbed.

Murad wound up the fishing line and put the hook in his coat pocket. There was blood on his ironed pants, and his shoes were covered with moss.

For a second, the crane just lay there. Then he scrambled to his feet and hopped out of the bushes. He suddenly looked gigantic. When he stood upright, he almost came up to my chin.

The young bird pattered along the shoreline in a bit of a daze. But there was no sign of any other cranes. He screeched so loud that it hurt.

Jadran looked very serious. "He's calling his family, isn't he?"

"They'll come looking for him," said Murad. "Animals don't just abandon their young."

We stood and watched for half an hour. It was starting to get dark, and the lake glowed one last time, a rusty orange. But the cranes didn't come back.

Every time the bird did a little jump, Jadran hopped along with him. When he tried to spread his wings, Jadran did the same. He stretched out one arm, with the other dangling limply beside his body.

Sprrrree! went the crane, as if it had swallowed a soccer referee's whistle. *Spri ri ri ree!*

"Sprig!" cooed Jadran. "Sprig! That's his name."

Mom bit her lip. We all knew what that meant. Everything that Jadran gave a name to had a special place in his head. And once it had a place there, it never left.

Jadran hopped about, flapping one arm. "His wing's broken, isn't it?"

"We'll have to call the park rangers," I said quickly. "They'll know what to do."

Murad wiped his shoes clean with one of Mom's tissues.

"That sounds like a smart idea," he said. "After all, it is a wild animal."

Jadran wasn't afraid of wild animals. Before anyone could say anything, he danced toward Sprig with big steps.

At that point, Mom lost what little was left of her good mood. Jadran had already given us enough headaches in the past few weeks.

"I'm going to look after him!" he said, stalking the bird like a dog.

"Stop it!" I shouted.

Jadran opened up his arms to make a trap and chased Sprig toward the jetty. Blocking Sprig's way with his foot, he grabbed the bird from behind. The bird just let himself be caught. Jadran slid an arm under him and picked him up. He stroked the bird's back, smoothing his feathers and folding the bird's legs into his hands.

"Quiet now, my little Sprig," he whispered. "I'm taking you home with me!"

The wind was blowing harder and harder. The hazel branches swished about, and dark clouds tumbled above the trees.

Mom and Murad discussed what to do.

"I'm out of here." Yasmin was talking half to her phone and half to us. She was already walking back to the path.

Jadran hugged Sprig to his chest.

"Don't squeeze him so hard, Giant. You'll suffocate him," said Mom.

"He's staying with me!"

For a moment, my gaze locked with Jadran's. And it was enough to convince me that we couldn't leave Sprig behind.

"When it's dark, a fox could get him," I said.

"Murad has a friend who's a vet," said Mom. "We'll take him to see her."

Murad nodded encouragingly. So that was the plan.

But Jadran didn't fit into any plans. He started to tremble frantically. His lips became thin. His chest was heaving up and down.

"Don't do it!" I pressed my hands to my ears.

Jadran opened his mouth wide. Sprig cowered as Jadran started howling fiercely. Mom glanced left and right. Luckily, there was no one else on the shore.

"Fine, then," she said quickly. "Take him home."

Jadran peeped with one eye. The howl was at half volume now.

"But tomorrow morning . . ."

Jadran wiped the tears from his face with his sleeve. He gave Sprig a stroke, rocked him like a giant baby, and then walked past Yasmin and into the woods.

Within three steps, he'd already forgotten that the world had just been about to end.

A YOUNG CRANE DOESN'T FIT into a laundry basket. Or even into the biggest of moving boxes. Mom didn't want Sprig in the bathroom or the hallway. With five of us, the apartment was already a tight fit.

And so he had to go on the balcony.

We put newspapers on the floor. Murad took our socks off the drying rack, tipped it on its side, and lifted it onto the railing. Then he tied it in place with a piece of clothesline to make a sort of cage, so Sprig couldn't fall down from the eighth floor.

Jadran went to look for some food for Sprig while the rest of us tried to take care of the bird's wound. Murad lifted up his wing, I pushed the fluffy down out of the way, and Mom sprayed some antiseptic on the place where the fishhook had been. The bleeding had stopped, and Murad said the wound wasn't so bad that it needed stitches.

Jadran had taken the bread crumbs off a fish stick and cut the fish into little pieces. He put some water in a plastic bowl and took it all out to the balcony. Then we let Sprig go. He flapped wildly against the railing before huddling up on the blanket we'd put in a corner for him.

We stood at the window watching him for quite a while. Murad and Mom were kind of clinging to each other. Jadran grabbed my hand and gave it a squeeze whenever Sprig made the slightest movement.

"He'll have covered everything in poop by tomorrow," grumbled Yasmin. "And with that drying rack, it's like a prison in here."

Then she disappeared into Jadran's room, which had been hers since they'd moved in, and slammed the door. She really should take down his poster of the Seven Dwarfs.

Down below, the city was going to sleep. The streets were emptying. The stores' shutters were dropping.

"You have to eat something," whispered Jadran. He opened the balcony door a crack and slid the plate with the chopped-up fish stick closer to the bird. "Go on. I cooked it for you."

Sprig didn't even look up.

"He's mad at me." Jadran thumped the door.

"Why?" I asked. "It wasn't you who left that fishhook lying around, was it?"

Jadran banged his forehead against the glass. "I chased his family away. And now he's all alone!"

"Not completely." I gave Jadran's back a rub.

He stuffed a chunk of fish stick into his own mouth.

We were sleeping right next to each other now. In my room there was just enough space for two mattresses, a chair to hang our clothes on, a little bookcase for my schoolbooks, and a wardrobe. When Jadran flailed in his sleep, he bashed me in the face. And he made weird rasping and rattling noises, like he was living every dream out loud.

But I still liked having him in my room. When I slept alone, I sometimes had nightmares. I'd dream that I'd gotten up in the morning and everyone had disappeared off the face of the earth.

"You're Jadran's guardian angel," Mom had told me when I was only eight. When I was writing my first book report, Jadran was still struggling away with his clumsy block letters. "If your brother's having problems, then you have to help him."

"Jadran's a giant," I said. "How am I supposed to help him?"

"You're a giant too, Josh. A little giant—on the inside."

"He's the strongest kid in the whole neighborhood. He beats everyone at arm wrestling and I . . ."

Mom just smiled and told me to take good care of him.

I slid even closer to Jadran and put my head on his belly. He didn't say anything, but I knew he was awake.

We were going to make a breathing bridge. We did it every night, or he couldn't get to sleep. I started and set the pace. As I breathed in deep, Jadran copied me.

In and out. Chest and belly.

Pffff.

My brother blew out over my chin.

The breathing game was actually Mom's idea. She and Jadran did it from when I was a baby. I used to lie between them in the big bed. They tried to breathe just as quickly as me and with the same puffs and grunts.

"Breathing together creates a bond," Mom would say. "A bond that's bigger and stronger than just that moment."

"Now you, Giant."

Jadran breathed in bursts, trembling. And I trembled with him. He let the air rush through his lips. And so I did the same, just as loud. But soon he was going way too fast.

"You're going to lose me," I whispered. "And then the whole bridge will break."

Jadran worked hard to get us back to the same rhythm.

"In," he panted. "In. In. In!"

I sucked in so much air that my lungs almost burst. And then, finally, we were back in sync. My head bounced along on Jadran's belly.

The little room, the apartment block, the murmur of the city—they were all gone. There was nothing but my brother and me, in that wonderful big bed.

JADRAN GOT UP TWICE IN the night to go see if Sprig was still there. He put his face right up to the balcony door and blew clouds on the glass. Getting him back to bed wasn't easy.

In the morning, he ate his cornflakes on the balcony. It was a disaster area. The newspapers had been shredded, Sprig had kicked over his water bowl, and there was bird poop all the way up the wall. But Jadran didn't care. He knelt by the door, with his breakfast bowl and spoon on the ground in front of him. The crane was trembling against the railing.

"Leave him," I said. "He's scared."

"He has to eat or he'll die." Jadran flicked a cornflake toward the bird with his spoon.

Sprig didn't catch it. But he did look up. And that was a start.

Jadran stayed on the balcony all morning. Mom didn't even try to convince him that we should take Sprig back. This way at least Jadran wasn't getting under her feet.

"Okay, then," she said, putting on her coat. "The crane can stay tonight." She linked arms with Murad, and they went out to buy new bed linen.

I looked it up on the internet for Jadran: Cranes are omnivores. They eat everything. During the breeding season, they mainly eat insects, worms, and frogs, but rarely fish. And when they're migrating, they scratch around empty fields for bits of leftover wheat and corn.

"You see? Cornflakes!" grinned Jadran. "Now we just need some worms."

We put on our shoes. Jadran grabbed a ladle and I took an empty jam jar from the kitchen cabinet.

I raced downstairs and outside. Jadran took the elevator. Mom didn't actually allow him to do it on his own. And certainly not as a race. But when she wasn't home, we did it anyway. I jumped up onto the handrail and slid down the rest of the staircase on my butt.

He was already waiting down in the entrance hall, looking very proud of himself.

In front of the apartment block there was a flower bed full of roses. Jadran began digging among the plants with the ladle. Lumps of soil flew all around. We collected some wood lice, centipedes, and earthworms from among the dry leaves. Jadran found a load of little bugs under a loose paving stone. Soon the jar was crawling with critters.

But when we wanted to go back upstairs, the door was shut—and we hadn't brought a key.

Jadran pressed the doorbell way too long.

"Yes?" crackled the intercom. Above the row of buttons, there was a speaker and a camera. Yasmin, upstairs in the apartment, could see on a screen who was ringing the doorbell.

"We can't get in!" I shouted.

Jadran pressed his nose to the lens.

"Step back so that I can see you better," said Yasmin.

"Sprig's hungry."

"You two are filthy." It didn't sound very friendly—and it wasn't.

"Open the door!" I hid my black fingers behind my back.

Jadran proudly lifted up the jar of wriggling critters.

Yasmin was not impressed. "You've done your jacket up wrong, Jadran."

He lowered the jar again and looked down.

"Leave him alone," I hissed. "Does it really matter?"

"And your hair's a complete mess."

I undid Jadran's buttons and put them in the right holes. Then I ran my fingers through my hair. "Better?"

Yasmin burst out laughing, as if it had all been a joke. The big door clicked open.

Feeding Sprig live worms was really gross. They struggled in his beak. He bit a centipede into two pieces before gobbling it down. Jadran put a shiny beetle on the palm of his hand and let it tumble to the ground in front of Sprig. There was no escape for them.

After twenty creepy-crawlies, Sprig looked a lot more comfortable. He fluffed up his feathers, scratched at the blanket with his feet, and settled down for a little nap.

Jadran copied him. He stood on one leg and pulled his neck in.

"Wake me up when Mom's back," he said.

"Want me to bring you some worms too?" I asked.

But Jadran had already started his crane nap.

I tiptoed back inside.

MURAD AND I WERE PLAYING *Flying Zombies*. I banged away on the keyboard and had already bagged ten zombies before Murad could even click the mouse once.

"The last one's yours," I said.

Murad blew up the entire zombie town.

"We should do this more often," he said.

Jadran didn't like the new sheets that Mom had bought. Just the smell was making him uneasy. He kept sneezing and kicking off the comforter.

"Come here," I whispered, patting the mattress beside me.

Jadran pushed his pillow next to mine and rolled up close to me. I didn't sleep a wink, but he snored away happily all night.

The next day, we taught Sprig his own name.

"Sprig," called Jadran. He was the daddy crane now, and he threw some grain onto the ground for his baby bird.

Pretty soon the bird came to us whenever we said his name. He was still too young to call like an adult bird, and just answered with a plaintive cry.

Spri-ri-ri-ree sprirrrreee.

"Sprig! Sprig!"

Taming the bird with Jadran was fun. My brother hadn't been in such a good mood for ages. He beamed when Sprig pecked the first bit of bread from his hand. And so Mom said Sprig could stay a little longer. His wound was healing quickly. Another few days and we'd take him back to the lake.

It wasn't long before Sprig started hopping around after us. When Mom wasn't looking, Jadran opened the balcony door, and he and Sprig strutted around the apartment. I gave Jadran instructions on how to do the best imitation of Sprig. He held his neck nice and straight, pulled in his tummy, and pattered about on his toes.

Sprig still couldn't fly yet, though. Or at least he didn't show any signs of wanting to. He didn't even try to open his wings.

"We have to teach him," said Jadran.

"We can't fly," I said. "And how can you teach someone something when you can't do it yourself?"

"If you *really* want to do it, you can do anything."

That, of course, was what they'd drummed into him at his special school. They gave Jadran an overdose of tips and compliments at the Space. And he was really, really good at endlessly repeating other people's sentences.

"We're way too heavy," I said.

Jadran zapped me with a glare. "We need wings!"

And Jadran didn't mean homemade paper or cardboard wings. He wanted big wings with real feathers.

He wanted Mom's blue wings.

She used to wear them when she was still performing in musicals with Dad. They were specially made to measure. But since Dad had left, she had wanted nothing more to do with them.

Jadran was already running into the hallway to fetch the key that hung above the shoe cabinet. But I stopped him. Mom kept her musical costumes in the basement. And even I wouldn't let him go down there on his own.

Mom didn't like going down into the basement. She said it was a kind of time-travel machine. Before she realized what she was doing, she'd open the wrong box and find herself in a previous life. One she thought she'd almost forgotten.

I slipped the key into my pocket and walked ahead of Jadran all the way downstairs. The basement stank of mold and mothballs. There was a long line of metal doors, but I knew exactly which one was ours.

The small storage room was packed to the ceiling with crates, boxes of yellowing paper, and stuff that looked like it had come straight from a thrift store. At the far end was a rack with a bunch of long, black garment bags.

"We should have asked Mom first," I said.

But Jadran was heading straight for the rack, beaming all over. He'd always been fascinated by Mom's musicals. Before Mom and Dad split up, he often used to go to their performances. He'd sit at the back of the theater and sing along to all the songs. He even knew all their lines by heart, Mom said, even though he only half understood them.

Jadran ran his fingers over the hangers.

"Do you know which one they're in?" I asked.

Jadran hesitated for a moment and then took a bumpy-looking bag off the rack. I opened the zipper for him. The tips of the wings burst through the opening, as if they'd been waiting all those years to get out. Jadran slid the wings out of the bag and walked with them down the hallway and up to the basement door. He held them under the light.

They were dyed the most beautiful blue I had ever seen. Hundreds of real feathers were sewn to a wire frame. There were really long flight feathers, gleaming smaller ones, and a whole bunch of silky-soft down on the underside.

Jadran blew off the dust. He pushed his fingers into the thick layers of feathers and stroked them flat. Then he lifted the wings onto his back and put his arms through the leather straps.

It was a strange sight: my big, tall brother with those graceful wings. But somehow, I thought, they kind of suited him. I buckled them up around his wrists. That meant Jadran could really flap them by moving his arms up and down. And that's exactly what he did. The wings swished all around.

He flew upstairs ahead of me. He whooshed along the hallway and into the living room. I ran after him, quickly trying to move all the breakable objects out of his way.

"Hey, boys, what's all this?" Mom jumped up from her chair when she saw the wings. The knife she was using to chop vegetables clattered onto the floor.

"I'll put them back in a bit," I said quickly.

But Mom didn't hear me. She was staring wide-eyed at Jadran, who was standing by the balcony window and flapping his wings.

"Up and down!" he shouted.

Every time he flapped the wings, Mom's head went back and forth, as if she was trying to shake off a bad memory. Then she bent down to pick up the knife and went on chopping broccoli.

The young bird stared at Jadran through the glass.

"Give him some food," I said. "Then he'll learn that it's fun."

And that was how we started the first flying lesson. Jadran showed him how, and I gave Sprig a beetle whenever he lifted his wings a bit. The injured wing was slower, but it still moved along with the other one.

"Up!" shouted Jadran.

And down went the beetles.

Yasmin stood in the doorway. Her bangs hung over the top of her glasses.

"Do you want to try?" asked Jadran. "You're a pretty mommy bird, Yaz." He ran around Yasmin, pushing out his butt like a big, feathery tail.

"Have you gone crazy?" She quickly stepped back

and slammed the balcony door. "You guys are such morons!"

"Yasmin, we don't say that kind of thing!" Murad called from the ironing board, with his pants in his hand. "Say sorry to them!"

But Yasmin didn't say anything at all.

Jadran lowered the wings. "Aren't they pretty, then?"

"They're beautiful, Giant," I said.

Inside the apartment, Murad ran after Yasmin to give her a roasting. She'd said we were morons. Both of us. It sounded so mean. It was completely untrue. But in a strange way I was relieved.

At least Yasmin hadn't treated my brother and me any differently.

THERE WAS A PATCH OF grass behind the apartment block. We wanted to take Sprig out there. The flapping was going better and better, so I thought he was ready to practice outside. Jadran had the blue wings on his back. He rattled a can of food, and the crane followed us to the elevator.

Sprig got one worm for each floor. He couldn't stop staring at the flickering lights.

On the fourth floor the elevator stopped. I pushed Sprig into a corner, and Jadran and I stood in front of him like a wall, as we'd agreed. We didn't want anyone to know we had a crane in the apartment.

Rafaela and her twins stepped in. She had one little kid on each hand.

"Good morning," said Jadran, overdoing the friendliness, as he tried to hide the bird behind his baggy pants. "And how are you today?"

Rafaela smiled, while her daughters looked in

terror at the winged giant who was blocking half the elevator.

"We're fine, Jadran. How about you guys?"

Rafaela loved my brother. She worked at the drugstore and sometimes she brought samples of toothpaste home for him, those mini-tubes with the new flavors.

"Great, thanks!" Jadran grinned and showed his teeth, so she could see that the toothpaste was working.

Sprig gave himself a scratch on the back of my jeans. I nearly had a heart attack.

"I bet you guys are really busy now, huh? I saw the moving truck. That Murad seems like a friendly man. And he has a nice daughter. Isn't she about your age, Josh?"

Ping! went the elevator.

The twins started arguing about who got to leave the elevator first.

"Those wings really suit you," Rafaela said to Jadran. She acted like she hadn't seen Sprig.

We waited until they were gone. Sprig hopped into the entrance hall after Jadran like a puppy dog. He slid about on the marble tiles and then scrambled outside onto the sidewalk.

"Good, Sprig, that's right. Come on!"

I walked ahead to make sure there was no one out on the grass.

"The coast's clear, Giant!" I shouted back around the corner.

Jadran wasn't walking with a hunched back now, but parading proudly along the strip of concrete beside the building, with his chin held high. I felt even smaller than usual.

Jadran gave me the can of food and sat down on a bench.

"Kroo kroo kroo!" he yelled, spreading his wings.

Sprig greedily pecked at a blob of mayonnaise beside the garbage can.

"Stop it! It'll make you sick!" I tried to drive the bird toward the bench, but he spotted a soggy bread crust on the ground.

That didn't put Jadran off. "Watch how I do it!" He bounced across the grass with the wings open.

Sprig dashed as quickly as he could in the opposite direction. Jadran swooped and flew after him.

"Stop!" I yelled.

But the daddy crane didn't understand that word. He raced to the bike shed on his long legs, chasing his chick into a corner.

"Come on, you can do it! You can do it!" he shouted, just like his counselors at the Space spoke to him.

I had to do something. Sprig was shivering and

shaking. Any minute now he'd escape, and he wouldn't last long in the city. I went and stood behind Jadran and tried to press his arms down. He tensed his muscles.

"You're going to frighten him," I said.

"He has to fly! After his family."

"You're going too fast." I snuggled against his back and stroked his shoulders until he finally stopped flapping. "It's like the breathing, Giant. You have to do it at his speed."

We used the can of food to lure Sprig away from the bike shed. It took ages to get him to jump up onto the bench. And once he was there, he didn't want to leave.

Jadran just went on flapping his wings. He darted across the grass and then skimmed over the ground like a fighter jet. But Sprig was not in the mood. Even when he tumbled off the back of the bench, he kept his wings closed.

"It's not high enough," said Jadran firmly.

It didn't work off the dumpster either. Jadran lifted Sprig onto it, but the lid was too slippery and Sprig almost went head over heels. Then Jadran wanted to clamber up onto the roof of the bike shed. I only just managed to stop him.

Then I saw him eyeing the side of the building.

Flapping and fluttering, he kept steering Sprig closer to that direction. I knew what he was trying to do. But that was not an option. No one was allowed on the fire escape. It was only there for emergencies.

"There!" Jadran pointed one wing at a metal platform halfway up the building, between the fourth and the fifth floors.

I shook my head. "Cranes always take off from the ground."

Jadran flapped his wings until the sweat was pouring down his forehead. Clouds of dust billowed up. He jumped as high as he could with his chunky calves. Sprig hopped about a bit, but he didn't fly.

Jadran's mouth became a tight line. "It's not working from the ground!"

"You need to have a bit more patience, Giant," I said. "Come on, let's go back inside. And we'll try again tomorrow."

Jadran didn't believe in tomorrow. For him, everything was *now*. He made a face and walked toward the fire escape. I ran after him and tugged on his sleeve.

"Stop it! Mom will be so mad if she sees you there!" And I didn't mean just mad at him. Mainly at me. If I couldn't stop it, then I was a lousy guardian angel.

Jadran didn't care about Mom getting mad. He pushed me away. And so I had to come up with something else.

My only options now were all bad ones.

I STOOD BETWEEN JADRAN AND the fire escape, the blades of grass nailing me to the spot. He waved his giant hands threateningly. But I didn't falter.

"Let me do it," I said. "I'm not as heavy as you and . . ."

"I'm not too heavy!" Jadran stuck his nose in the air like a beak. He pulled in his stomach until he was all ribcage.

"Give me the wings."

Jadran peeped at me out of the corner of his eye. "You gonna take Sprig with you?" His hands dropped back beside his body.

I nodded and undid the buckles around his wrists. Jadran slid the wings off his back and ran off to grab the crane. Mom's wings were way too big for me. The biggest feathers came down to my knees.

But there was no way back.

We agreed that Jadran would wait at the bottom while I climbed up the fire escape, wearing the blue wings. I clasped one hand around the cold metal and hugged Sprig to me with the other hand. His long neck got in the way and he kicked out viciously, but I didn't let go.

Rung by rung, I found my foothold. The wind blew under Mom's wings, wafting the feathers into my face.

Don't look down, I thought. It'll soon be over.

My legs were wobbling. From down there, it hadn't looked that high, but when I reached the platform, I felt dizzy. I put Sprig down and held onto the railing.

"Giant?" I yelled down. "I made it!"

But there was no answer and no sign of anyone on the grass. Down on the street, a motorbike roared past.

That was when I felt the ladder shaking. Beneath me, I heard a rasping, panting sound.

"Pff!" Jadran stuck his head up over the edge of the platform. His face was red, and sweat was running down it. "It's high up here, huh?"

I took a step to one side and wanted to yell that he hadn't kept our agreement and that he had to go back down right now. But I didn't dare. Every word could be the wrong one, the spark that lit his fuse.

I thought of what I'd seen Mom do so many times before: close her eyes for a count of three, take a deep breath, and then try to persuade him as calmly as possible.

"Hold on with both hands, Giant."

Sprig wasn't scared of heights. His sharp claws tapped on the metal.

"You have to move the wings," said Jadran, "so that Sprig can see how."

"That's too dangerous up here," I said.

"Then I'll do it." Jadran grabbed my arm and started to unbuckle the wings.

"Stop it!" I pulled away and stepped to the edge. I stretched my arms beside me.

Jadran pushed Sprig toward me, giving him a pep talk. "Look, my little birdie. This is how to fly. Open your wings and then jump. Got it?" And to me he said, "Up and down, Josh. Keep moving them up and down."

It was such a horribly long way down, and keeping those huge wings open was hard.

"That's enough," I whispered. "Sprig gets it now."

"He doesn't get anything!"

"Maybe he's not ready yet."

Jadran stamped angrily on the platform. "You have to try harder, Josh!"

At that moment, I heard shouting from below. I looked down and saw Yasmin running across the grass, apparently searching for us. She looked behind the bike shed, and turned around and peered up when she heard the thumping of Jadran's feet. Her mouth fell open.

"What are you two doing up there?" she shouted.

I closed the wings and took a step back.

"Sprig's going to fly!" shrieked Jadran. "Look!"

Sprig was standing beside me. And finally he was copying me.

He opened up the injured wing.

"You see!" Jadran's deep voice echoed off the buildings. "I told you so! I always tell you so, don't I?"

Sprig spread his wings wider than ever before. His body swayed in the wind, and it looked like he was about to be lifted up into the air.

Yasmin waved at us. "Your mom's home. What if she sees you guys up there?"

"Come on, Jadran," I mumbled. "Let's go have something to eat." Mom could even get him out of the bathtub with that.

Pwee ee ee! Sprig hopped over the platform, beating his wings. *Pwee ee!*

"He's almost flying," hissed Jadran. "We can't stop now."

I closed my eyes again, counted to three, and went and stood next to Sprig. Jadran mustn't explode. Not here, not three stories above the ground.

I swallowed. "One more time. Then we'll go back down. Promise?"

Two pairs of wings opened up.

"More!" screamed Jadran. "Faster, little one!"

He came and stood right behind me and Sprig. I could feel his breath on the back of my neck. I waved the blue wings one last time.

"No!" screamed Yasmin.

"See? You can do it!" Jadran cried triumphantly. "If you *really* want to do it, you can do anything!"

And then he gave me such a shove that I plummeted down from the platform to the ground below.

Hang-Glider

THE BED, THE TWO CHAIRS, and the closet—everything was white. The curtains were green, but the sky behind them was a bright white sheet too.

"Would you like some water?" asked Mom.

I wasn't thirsty. I was still too drowsy from the anesthetic.

Mom gave me the outline of what had happened: I'd fallen three stories down. I lay on the grass, looking like I was dead, and Yasmin ran off crying and looking for help. Meanwhile Jadran went crazy. They'd had to drag him in through a window on the fourth floor.

"I murdered him!" he was bellowing when the ambulance came racing onto our street with its lights flashing. "I murdered my brother!"

It took four paramedics to get me onto the stretcher while trying to calm Jadran down. Luckily they had medication, said Mom, because words weren't enough to stop him. The pills gave Jadran a thick tongue and zombie eyes.

I was taken to the hospital in the ambulance. They'd operated on my leg for hours, and then I'd slept almost around the clock.

"Did Sprig fly?" My voice sounded hoarse and far away, as if someone else was speaking.

Mom sighed a dark cloud into the room. "Three times around the grass, Yasmin says."

Dr. Mbasa was standing in the doorway.

"You were very lucky, Josh." She was smiling the way doctors sometimes do, with a kind mouth in a stern face. "Your spine isn't damaged. And you still have your legs."

My legs.

I slid my hand under the sheet and felt a thin hospital gown and a whole load of dressings and bandages. There was a plaster cast on my right leg from my groin to my calf. My left ankle was wrapped up tightly.

"Three breaks and a miracle," whispered Mom.

"I'll bring you the wheelchair tomorrow," said Dr. Mbasa. "And then we'll do a lot of practice. Believe me, I'm going to make a wheelchair champion out of you."

My skin twitched under the plaster. Mom said they'd given me twelve stitches.

"When will I be able to walk again?" I asked.

"A bit of patience," said Dr. Mbasa. "After the winter you'll be running to school again."

"But that's months away!"

I could tell from Mom's face that she thought it was too long as well, but she didn't say anything. She stood up and put a pillow behind my back.

At six o'clock, Murad and Yasmin came to take over from Mom. Jadran was still in the car and didn't want to get out.

"Hi," said Murad.

And "Hi," said Yasmin.

I didn't say hi back.

Yasmin hung her wool scarf over the radiator. The whole room smelled of wet sheep.

"I brought some goodies," said Murad, conjuring up one caramel candy after another.

Mom went to get coffee. She gave Murad the plastic cup and moved a chair next to the head of my bed. She patted the seat with her hand to make it clear that he had to sit there.

"I'm just going to go see Jadran in the car. I'll call you later, Little Giant." Mom gave me such a big kiss that it felt like she'd be away for years.

Yasmin fiddled with her jacket. She stared at the bump of the plaster cast under the sheet. Her bangs had been trimmed. There was almost an inch between her black hair and her eyebrows now.

"Does it hurt?" she asked.

I shrugged.

"I dreamed about you last night," said Yasmin. "You were wearing those wings and you took off like a rocket."

We drank lukewarm hospital water and chewed Murad's candies. I noticed that Yasmin kind of rolled her lips up at the corners when she ate, and I caught myself thinking that I actually quite liked it.

"I put those wings in your room," she said. "Your mom wanted to throw them out, but I thought . . ."

I had candy stuck in my teeth. So I smiled with my mouth closed.

Murad came and sat a little closer to me. Out in the corridor, the nursing cart rattled past.

"Are you very mad at Jadran?" he asked.

"He's my brother," I said.

"I think I'd be furious. But you seem to be keeping pretty calm."

I didn't feel calm at all. Crushed would be a better word. I put one hand on my tummy. It was hard and cold, as if the plaster had spread from my leg and up over my belly button.

"Jadran thought I could fly," I said.

Murad frowned. There were grey hairs in his eyebrows.

"I don't think things can be easy for you, Josh," he said. "Jadran is sometimes so . . ."

"Happy!" I said quickly. I hated it when people talked about Jadran like he was some kind of problem we had to work together to find a solution for.

"Yep, he's often happy," said Murad with a smile. "But when he's not, you can always come to me and . . ."

I felt like a mummy made out of plaster. Murad took a swig of my water and put his hand on the bed, right next to mine.

"Did you know that cranes do really disgusting burps?" I said.

MURAD SLEPT OVER AT THE hospital. Not that it was necessary, but he really wanted to. He sat on one chair and put his legs up on another one with a blanket over him.

I thought about Jadran, lying at home all alone in my room. They'd probably given him more pills to calm him down. Later, when Murad was asleep, I'd try to breathe toward Jadran. Maybe our breathing bridge would work at a distance too.

An ambulance's siren wailed outside. Blue streaks flashed on the curtains. Murad wriggled his feet under the blanket. I squashed my thoughts into earplugs and closed my eyes.

In the morning my sheets were all tangled up. Murad was pretty impressed that I managed to do that with my leg in plaster. A nurse opened the curtains and gave me my painkillers. Then I got breakfast in bed, with a heated-up croissant.

There seemed to be no end to the rest of the day. At eight o'clock, Murad left for work and Mom took over. She didn't leave me alone for five minutes. She went with me to all the tests, with me in my underpants and hospital gown, and her in her coat, which was way too hot.

Mom nodded as if she already knew it all when she looked at the new X-rays with Dr. Mbasa. There were three steel pins and a few bolts in my leg. I'd never make it through a metal detector again without setting it off.

In the afternoon, Jadran finally came to visit. Mom had gone to fetch him from the Space. It was actually supposed to be a vacation week for the day students, but Jadran was allowed to go because of the accident. He worked in the garden and on the farm, together with the young residents who lived there permanently. I heard his footsteps thudding along the corridor. He banged the door open and thumped into the room.

In a single jump, he thudded onto my bed. The whole thing creaked. I only just got my leg out of the way in time.

"You're still alive," he panted.

"Yes," I said. "I'm still alive." If he'd hugged me any harder, they'd have had to operate on my ribcage.

We ate some of the candies. Well, I had one, and Jadran gobbled down all the rest.

"Sorry, sorry, sorry," he mumbled before every one.

The door swung open.

"Ta-daaa!" said Dr. Mbasa, as if she was bringing me a present. She pushed a little wheelchair decorated with two stickers of flames into the room. It was shining like new, and it smelled of disinfectant.

It looked so childish.

Maybe Mom should have warned Dr. Mbasa. The doctor obviously had no idea how Jadran might react when he saw me in a wheelchair. She didn't know that Jadran's giant body was so fragile on the inside.

Jadran quickly scrambled down from the bed and went and stood in the corner of the room, like a little kid who's just been told off. Dr. Mbasa showed Mom how to help me into the wheelchair. It seemed simple, but Mom made a big deal of it. She did everything way too carefully, as if I might fall apart.

Jadran's rasping breath was getting shallower and faster.

"Calm down, Giant," whispered Mom when I was finally sitting in the wheelchair.

I stayed there while Mom and Dr. Mbasa went out to talk in the corridor. I joked to Jadran that if they wanted to hide, they'd better not go to the ICU, but Jadran didn't get it. He was trying to fix a jacket button that had come loose and was dangling from a thread.

"Do you want me to do it for you?" I asked.

The thread snapped. The button rolled under the bed.

"I murdered you." Jadran was shaking. "I murdered your legs!"

I wanted to give him a hug, but the wheels were in the way.

He started banging the back of his head on the wall. "Sorry, sorry, sorry."

Bang, bang, bang!

Every sorry was a mark on the white of the room.

I didn't know what to say, because of course this time it really *was* Jadran's fault, even if he did believe that I'd fly.

"It's okay, Giant," I said. "I'm not mad at you. Really."

Jadran rammed the bed. His elbow knocked my

gym bag full of clothes onto the floor. And then he was gone.

"Sorry, sorry." He hurtled down the corridor.

"Where are you off to?" I heard Mom calling after him.

"Sorry, sorry, sorry."

The door to the stairs slammed behind him.

JADRAN WAS MISSING. THEY SEARCHED for him all evening and all night. Mom scoured the city, while Yasmin kept watch at home. They searched all the places my brother liked to go, the store with the cuckoo clock in the window, the bicycle bridge by the station, and the Japanese garden next to the library.

But Jadran was nowhere to be found. And so first they called in the counselors from the Space, and then the police.

They'd promised the night nurse would come let me know if there was any news. But no one came. And the night was empty and eerily quiet.

I lay on my back and stared up at the ceiling. I made a breathing bridge without knowing where the other side was.

Even before breakfast, Mom was standing beside my bed. Her eyes were puffy. She did her best to reassure me.

"Have another good think," she said. "He must have gone somewhere he knows. There must be something we're missing."

"The geese in the park," I said. "That house with those weird gargoyles, the fountain where he always tries to fish out the coins."

But they'd been everywhere.

Mom helped me into the wheelchair. She wanted to go for a coffee in the cafeteria. It wasn't as bitter as the coffee from the machine. She sat on one of the orange chairs and pulled me as close as possible.

"He'll manage just fine," I said as she ran her fingers through my hair.

"The three of us always manage just fine," she said, more to herself than to me.

Murad called every fifteen minutes. Yasmin sent a photo of Jadran that the police could use in the missing person report, if that proved necessary.

I rested my head on Mom's shoulder. She smelled a bit sweaty, but still good, like the flowery perfume that she sometimes dabbed on her neck. Mom nervously stroked my plaster cast. Like she thought it was her own leg.

I suddenly thought of a funny story that Jadran had once told me. Maybe it would cheer her up a bit.

"Do you remember that time Dad had been walking around looking for Jadran for hours?" I asked. "Dad was in a real panic. But Jadran had been hiding in a sleeping bag under your bed the whole time."

Mom had forgotten. She hardly ever remembered anything that involved Dad.

The phone call we'd been hoping for didn't come until eleven o'clock: Jadran had been found and he was all in one piece! I was so happy that I rang the nurses' bell three times. When Mom started crying, I buried my face in her soft tummy.

Jadran had walked all the way to the cranes' lake, almost ten miles away. He must have followed exactly the same route we'd driven a few days before: around the ring road, through the industrial park, and then along the winding road into the woods.

I thought about how bad Jadran must have felt last night—in the dark, with that cold wind in his face, and all those strange sounds he was so scared of, too scared to stop walking.

Near the lake was a bird-watching hut and a small visitors' center. Jadran had headed inside because he was hungry. He was wet and chilled to the bone. The woman who worked there as a nature guide had given him some crackers and instant soup out of a packet. When Jadran confessed that he'd nearly murdered his brother, she called the police.

Mom put on her coat and wanted to set off as quickly as possible.

"Tell him they're letting me go home tomorrow," I said. "And that I'm truly not mad at him."

She did her best to look cheerful.

Mom told me later that she spent almost two hours trying to persuade Jadran to go with her. But he wouldn't budge. He wouldn't get into her car and he wouldn't leave the visitors' center either. He just kept staring at the TV screen. There was a documentary on about cranes and their seasonal migration.

Mika, Jadran's personal counselor at the Space, was brought in to persuade him. He was crazy about her. He wrote her letters, sometimes as long as half a page, and said that he was going to marry her one day.

But not even Mika could get him to move.

"I want my brother," whispered Jadran. "My brother and no one else."

Dr. Mbasa wasn't at all happy that I was leaving the hospital a day early. They were planning more tests and X-rays. But luckily Mom was able to talk her into it. When Jadran got an idea in his head, everything else had to give way—that was how it had always been.

The doctor insisted on personally packing my bag and walking me to the exit. I was wearing an old pair of Jadran's sweatpants, which were baggy enough to fit my plaster cast.

"Don't forget to think about yourself too," she said as Murad drove toward us. "Your brother's very special, of course. But so are you, Josh."

Dr. Mbasa took me in her strong arms and lifted me into the car. Even with the passenger seat all the way back, my plastered leg only just fit in. She slid the folded-up wheelchair into the trunk and gave Murad the prescription for my medication. He had to promise her that he'd be really careful with me.

A HANG GLIDER FLEW LOW OVER the lake. It had three wheels, a motor with a huge propeller at the back, and triangular wings made of sailcloth. The sun gleamed on the pilot's white helmet.

But the most interesting thing was the young cranes. In a wide letter *V*, they flew after the hang glider, like it was the leader of the group. They didn't seem afraid of the motor's noise and, without hesitation, they followed every move that the aircraft made.

"There you are! Finally!" shouted Jadran as I rolled the wheelchair at full speed toward the TV screen he'd been watching all that time.

I hugged him.

I cuddled him.

I thumped his chest and told him he was a jerk for leaving me behind in the hospital like that.

He put his finger to his lips and pointed at the screen. "Now you can see it for yourself, Josh. That's how they do it!"

The hang glider flew higher above a bare, grassy landscape. Pictures filmed from the ground alternated with close-ups of young cranes in the air. Now you could really see how big their wings were. The sun glistened on their silver-brown backs as they slowly glided after the aircraft.

Jadran looked pretty rough, and drool was dripping from the corner of his mouth. But his eyes were gleaming.

"Do you get it, Josh?" he asked. "You get it now, huh?"

I did my best to follow him.

"Those young cranes don't have any parents. They're just like Sprig," I said. "Is that what you mean?"

Jadran nodded eagerly. "They can't leave without a dad or a mom. They don't know the way to Spain."

"And so that man's teaching them which direction to fly in?"

The pilot put the hang glider back on the ground. The cranes landed next to him on the grass. Their first flying lesson had gone well. In a few weeks' time, they'd begin their trek south together.

Jadran nudged me. "He's feeding them. Look!"

"That's their reward," I said.

The pilot had put an imitation crane's head over his arm. It had beady eyes, a plastic beak, and a patch of red, just like the adult birds. He pecked at the food with the head, as if he really was one of the cranes. It looked a bit creepy—a guy in a weird white helmet with a bird arm—but the young birds seemed used to it. They made the same trilling little squeaks as Sprig.

"They think he's their daddy," said Jadran.

The nature guide turned off the TV set.

"He must have watched that video thirty times already," she said to Mom. "No idea why."

"We visited here in spring," said Mika behind me. I recognized her sweet but kind of raspy voice immediately. "We watched that video then too. He must have remembered it."

Of course he did, I thought. Jadran remembers everything. He even remembers the last mile count he saw on the dashboard of Dad's car.

Now he looked at my leg and poked the plaster with his finger. "Sorry."

"It's okay, Giant. The doctor says I'll make a complete recovery."

"Sorry, sorry, sorry."

"Come on," I said. "We have to go home. Sprig's waiting for you."

"It's all my fault, isn't it?"

"Yes, you're right," I said to shut him up. "This time it really is all your fault."

And then Jadran finally stood up.

"You see!" he said. His pants were torn and there was a dark stain on his butt. "Can I push the wheelchair?"

The way home seemed endless. Jadran was silent, but his brain was sparking away. For once I was glad that I couldn't look inside his head.

It was too cramped on the back seat for my plaster cast, but Jadran still insisted that I should sit beside him. Mom and Murad had pushed their own seats as far forward as possible. Mom's knees were almost touching the steering wheel, and Murad was squeezed up against the glove compartment.

"It was smart of you, going into that hut, Giant," he said.

It sounded strange to hear Murad calling my brother that. Some words don't fit right in other people's mouths. "Giant" had always been a word for just Mom and me.

"You could have starved to death. Out in the woods in this cold."

"I got soup," said Jadran. "I never eat soup in the morning!"

Mom laughed. "And even Mika was there."

"Yes, Mika!"

She had been Jadran's personal counselor for two years now. And in those two years she had gotten him to do more than anyone else ever had. Jadran even put his own dirty work clothes in the washing machine at the Space. He could iron his shirts and pants perfectly by himself. And Mika had even taught him to drive the tractor, which he loved. He wanted to mow the lawn and plow the potato field all day long.

"You can imagine how worried she was when she heard you'd run away," said Mom. "You gave us a real fright, Jadran!"

Murad parked the car close to the front door of the apartment block. The roses brushed against the bumper. Mika had stopped by too. She had some things to discuss with Mom. And Jadran was insisting on showing her our bedroom, with the two mattresses on the floor.

Murad took the wheelchair out of the trunk, and Mika helped me out of the back seat. You could tell she'd done this loads of times before. Although she was slender, she easily lifted me out of the car and into the wheelchair. On her wrist there was a tattoo of a wolf.

"Wow! Well, I am stoked," she said. "So pumped this all turned out okay. And it's thanks to you, Josh.

If you hadn't come so quickly, we'd still be there now. We can nag as much as we like, but when it comes down to it, Jadran only listens to you." She pretended to look jealous and gave me a high five.

I could understand why my brother was so crazy about her.

Jadran ran into the hallway and pressed our bell three times.

"Is that you, Jadran?" Yasmin's voice crackled through the intercom's little speaker. "Turn around!"

Jadran did a half pirouette and pressed his face up to the camera.

"Open up!" he shouted. "Josh is here with his broken leg. And Mika wants to see my room!"

"Then get yourselves up here quickly," said Yasmin, as sweet as pie, and the glass door clicked open. "I missed you guys so much!"

I waved at the camera. For just a second, I believed she meant it.

MOM OPENED UP A PACKET of waffle cookies and put some on a plate. Jadran instantly grabbed two and stuffed them into his mouth. Sprig stood at the balcony door, pecking on the glass.

"How cute!" Mika squeaked. "He's talking to you, Jadran."

Mom shook her head. "We should never have brought that creature home."

Jadran opened the balcony door a bit. Sprig instantly stuck his head through.

Mika jumped back. "Whoa, I didn't know he was so big!"

"He won't hurt you." Jadran dug a dead dung beetle out of his pocket. "Look, Sprig, this is for you. From the woods." Then he took Mika's hand. "You coming? You promised!" He pulled her along the hallway to the bedrooms.

"Wow," I heard her shout, and then: "Hey, cool poster! The Seven Dwarfs!"

Mom went into the kitchen to fetch some tea. I nibbled at my waffle cookie, square by square. I could hear Jadran chattering away in the hallway. Now that she was finally here, Mika had to see everything: our room, his old room, the bathroom, the storage closet.

"It's so cozy here," she said, her laughter filling the apartment. "Like little sparrows, all snuggled up together."

The teacups rattled on Mom's tray. She put it down on the coffee table, but she didn't pour the water yet.

After the tour, Mom helped Jadran take a shower. Wearing his favorite sweatpants, he flopped onto the sofa and dug around in the packet of waffle cookies. Mika picked the crumbs off his sweater and gave him a picture book from her bag, so he'd have something to read while we talked.

She said, "I have a proposal for you."

Mom stood behind the sofa, waiting expectantly and drawing lines in the corduroy with her nails.

"Tomorrow I'll have a long talk about it with Jadran," Mika continued. "But first I want to hear what you guys think."

Murad stood up and poured everyone a cup. The tea bags floated for a moment on the steaming water before sinking.

"Jadran is sweet, and he tries to do things well," said Mika. "But he's also very unpredictable, and his body's getting big and strong. Too strong for you to handle him on your own. And after what's happened the past few days . . ."

Mika smiled sweetly at Jadran, who was completely wrapped up in the book, but her eyes were sad. I hardly dared to look at her.

"I had a discussion with the management this afternoon. There's a room for him at the Space. Jadran knows most of the other guys who live at the center. He'll be in a friendly community where he'll fit in well. We have specialist staff and all the care he needs."

"I'm not sure I understand," said Mom.

The teaspoons tapped out of sync.

"If you agree, he can move in this weekend."

It wasn't plaster around my leg. It was lead. And it was getting heavier and heavier. Any heavier and I'd sink through the floor, down through all those stories and into the basement.

"Of course we don't agree!" I blurted before I disappeared into the depths. "Jadran and I have never been apart for more than two nights. And now he's supposed to move out?"

Mika calmly stood up and crouched beside the wheelchair. The wolf on her arm was close to me. It was tilting its head and pricking up its ears.

"I get it, Josh," she whispered. "I really do. This seems really terrible now. Unbearable. But you'll see . . ."

I turned my head away. Murad had gone to stand by Mom behind the sofa. That was kind of him, because she looked like she was about to collapse.

"This isn't what I'd imagined," mumbled Mom, as she brushed the marks out of the fabric. "I hoped Jadran would always be able to stay here. I did everything I could, and now this . . ."

"No one ever imagines something like this," said Mika. "You've just got to make the best of it."

She went and sat back down beside Jadran on the sofa. He wasn't even listening to what was being said. He put down the book, grabbed the sugar bowl, and dumped three more spoonfuls into his cup.

Mom gulped, stretched her back, and forced a smile, as if she was suddenly ashamed of what she'd said before.

"You've already done so much to help us, Mika," she said. "And Jadran admires you. If you really think this is the only solution . . . you know, to Jadran's upset about the changes in our home and . . . the accident."

Mika gave my brother a cuddle. "We'll totally pamper him. As usual, huh, Jadran?"

That made him blush.

"And when is he allowed to come home?" asked Murad.

"Only on weekends at first. Later maybe a bit more often, and he can come stay with you during the vacations. But it has to be very clear to him, right from the start, that the Space is his new home."

Jadran took a swig of tea, but he was too greedy and burned his lips. He sprayed it all over the table.

"Oh, Jadran. What a mess!" Mom quickly fetched a dish towel, dabbed his mouth, and wiped the table. She hung the towel over the radiator and came to stand by my wheelchair. That was when I knew it was serious.

"Mom? You're not really going to send him away, are you?"

She shrugged. Her chest moved with her shoulders, but her heart stayed right where it was.

"We'll do it this way for now," she said.

Never, I thought. Never, never, never! I wanted to roll away, away from the living room, away from this terrible conversation.

But Mom put the brake on the wheelchair.

Jadran didn't have a brake. And right then he didn't really understand what was looming over him.

Mika was going to pamper him even more, yes!

He could go on the tractor with her more often, hooray!

He raced to the kitchen and took a bottle of soda from the cupboard.

"Soda fountain! The loudest one wins!" he yelled, pushing a full cup into my hand.

There we were, two brothers who always did everything together. Mom hid in Murad's arms. Yasmin sneaked off to her room. Mika was the only one who dared to look me in the face.

"To us!" shouted Jadran, raising his cup in the air. "To all of us!"

We both took a big gulp at the same moment, looked up, and gargled until the soda sprayed from our mouths.

Mom gave me a painkiller and helped me use the bathroom, because that was the trickiest thing about my leg. The whole time, we didn't say a word.

Jadran slid his mattress a little more firmly against mine and plumped up his pillow before he lay down. We'd be sleeping together another two nights. But as of Sunday, everything was going to change.

I was just about to begin a superstrong, indestructible breathing bridge when Yasmin pushed the door open a little.

"Are you asleep yet?" she asked.

Like that was possible within ten seconds. I flicked the nightlight back on.

"I just wanted to say that I think it's bad too," she said.

Jadran was lying on his back. He blinked in the bright light.

"It's not bad," I snapped. "It's terrible!"

I hoped Yasmin would slam the door now and leave us alone. But she didn't move. Jadran pushed the comforter off. The sleeves of his pajamas were too short. But Mom wasn't allowed to throw them out because they had Mickey Mouse on them.

"What's terrible?" he asked.

"That you're moving," said Yasmin.

I propped myself up on one elbow so that I could see her better. Without her glasses, her eyes didn't look as dark.

"You guys just moved." Jadran licked his cracked lips. "Not me."

"That's what Mika said, isn't it?" The corners of Yasmin's mouth were quivering. "Didn't you hear her?"

"Shh," I went. "Leave him alone. He needs to sleep. We'll talk to him about it tomorrow."

Jadran grabbed my wrist. "Mika's nice. She likes our room. Like sparrows, she said. We live like sparrows, all snuggled up together."

"I bet they have a nice room for you at the Space," said Yasmin.

I could have strangled her. This was not the moment to explain to Jadran what exactly was going on. He started to tremble.

"Guillaume sleeps at the Space," he said. "And Dewi and Sarah-with-an-*h*."

Yasmin took a step forward but I glared her back to the doorway. If she and Murad hadn't moved in, Jadran wouldn't have gotten so upset, and then this would never have to happen. Mom would calm my brother down, tell him it wasn't going to come to that. She could turn even the very worst of things into soft little words when she talked with her whipped-cream voice.

"Another two nights," I said to Jadran, because now I couldn't keep quiet any longer. "You'll be sleeping here another two nights. And then you'll get your own room at the Space."

Jadran pressed his forehead to mine. "Are you coming with me?"

His brain was boiling. And I had to boil with it.

"I'm staying here," I said.

The trembling became shaking. Our heads banged together.

"Me too," he said. "I'm staying here too."

We held our breath at the same moment. Yasmin mumbled something and shut the door. Jadran sank down onto the mattress.

"Come on, let's go to sleep now, Giant," I whispered, trying to turn onto my side toward him. "Mika will explain everything to you tomorrow."

I blew out over his face.

Then he exploded.

Mom's blue wings were hanging over the chair behind my mattress. Jadran leaped up and grabbed them. He lifted them over his head. They cast a shadow on the bed. He put his arms through the leather straps and opened the wings up wide. The flight feathers swished against the wallpaper. The light swung frantically back and forth. My schoolbooks tumbled off the shelves.

"Don't do that, Jadran!" Because of my dumb leg I couldn't even stand up to stop him.

Jadran couldn't hear me anymore. He was jumping around and smashing into the walls like a wild bird in a cardboard box.

"Giant, put those wings back!" I breathed as calmly as possible. Maybe he'd join in.

Jadran looked at me. For one heartrending moment. Then he pulled the wings apart. Hundreds of feathers swirled around the room. It was one gigantic blue cloud. And in that cloud Jadran stood tugging at the wire frame. He tugged off the down and tossed it up high. He tore off the feathers and threw them all around. One by one, all the long flight feathers went into the air.

"Stop!" I screamed. "You're ruining them!"

But Jadran still hadn't had enough. He wheeled

the bare wings around. He bashed the ceiling and flailed at the walls. He chased after the feathers and batted them back up high before they touched the floor.

It was like a kind of fight. A fight against something that was lighter than nothing. Something that no one could grasp. The feathers whirled around Jadran's head like a flock of blue birds.

If he opened his mouth right now, he'd choke on them.

THE BEDROOM WAS FULL OF feathers. But Mom didn't ask any questions. She shook out the comforters and picked the down from my hair. She swept everything into a heap. Then she lifted me into the wheelchair and pushed me into the living room.

Yasmin put the breakfast bowls on the table. She looked kind of messy with her hair down. But nicely messy, I thought.

Jadran was rocking uneasily back and forth. A drowsy fly had been lured out of its hiding place by the warmth of the heating, and it was buzzing against the kitchen light. I stuffed my mouth full of cornflakes so that I didn't have to say anything.

"Enjoying your breakfast?" Murad ventured.

Mom tipped the blue feathers back into the dusty garment bag, which she'd fetched from the basement. She pulled so hard on the zipper that it seemed like she wanted to never be able to open it again.

At half past eight, Mom took Jadran to the Space. She and Mika were going to talk it all through with him. And he could take a look at his room. Tonight he'd sleep at home for the last time, and tomorrow we'd move his things for good.

My stomach cramped up when I thought about it, and Jadran was dreading it too. He froze in the hallway and then pressed all the elevator buttons. He didn't agree to go until Mika called and asked if he wanted to go on the tractor with her after their discussion.

I retreated to the balcony. The wheelchair only just fit, and the wheels were soon covered in bird poop. Sprig was sitting on his blanket with his legs folded under the warm down on his belly. I gave him a worm and stroked his head, just where the first few black feathers were growing.

"Giant's leaving tomorrow," I said. "And then we're taking you back."

Sprig swallowed the worm in one bite. I clenched my fingers around the railing. The rain blew cold against my cheeks.

When you can't talk things out, you have to walk them off. That's what Mom always used to say when we'd been waiting for hours on our bench at the children's hospital yet again. Jadran had to go there for all kinds of tests, so that the doctors could figure out in actual numbers what exactly was different about him. What percentage he was ordinary and what percentage he was extraordinary.

While we were waiting, Mom used to take me outside and we'd go for a walk. Every step was a word, every sidewalk was a sentence. It didn't improve our conversations any, but we never got lost.

Now I couldn't walk. And talking to Mom was completely impossible. It wasn't just my legs that were broken, it was our words too.

"There's no need for us to worry. Jadran's going to be okay," she said when she got home. "He's getting the room next to Guillaume's. He has a TV and his own bathroom."

I was playing Battleship with myself on a sheet of graph paper. Mom opened her laptop. Her fingers rested on the keyboard but they didn't move.

Yasmin came and joined us at the table. She was making flowers out of crepe paper, and before long she had a whole pile of them.

"For the party," she said.

"What party?" I aimed a bomb and put a cross in the sea. *X*.

"For tomorrow," said Yasmin. "When Jadran leaves! We have to do something, don't we?"

"You don't have a party because someone's going away, do you?" I fired again and sank a battleship. *XXX*. I won and lost at the same time.

"Take it easy, Josh. You know that Yasmin means well." Mom closed her laptop and came and stood behind me. "Maybe we should all make a bit more of an effort."

"An effort? What for?" I leaned forward and put my head on my arms.

But Mom wasn't going to be put off. She rubbed her hands warm and massaged my shoulder blades, exactly in the spot where angels' wings grow.

"For each other," she said. "We need to be kind to each other."

All that massaging was getting on my nerves. I shoved the wheelchair backward and banged into her hips.

"And what about Jadran?" I yelled. "Do you call that kind? You're just abandoning him!"

Mom took hold of my arm and firmly rolled me back. "I'm not abandoning anyone!"

"So why are you putting him in an institution?"

Mom hadn't expected that. She sighed herself inside out.

"That does sound pretty cold," she said. "But it's

not cold at the Space at all. Jadran's going to be in a community with other nice young people like him. It's the best solution now. For us, for Murad and Yasmin. But for him too!"

She was talking very calmly, to make sure every word went in. But to me it sounded more fake and two-faced than ever.

After lunch I did Dr. Mbasa's exercises, and then I was supposed to rest. Mom helped me lie down on the sofa and put the box of painkillers on the table for me. While I was sleeping, she went into town to buy an alarm clock for Jadran.

Mom had pulled the door shut behind her for just a minute when the bell rang. Yasmin came into the room, looking annoyed, and peered at the screen of the intercom.

"It's Jadran!"

"What's he doing here?" I pulled myself up on the back of the sofa, so that I could look at the screen too. All I could see was a gigantic nose. "Mom was supposed to be picking him up later, wasn't she?"

"Quick!" yelled Jadran. "Open the door!"

There was hay on his jacket, and he was wearing his rubber boots. He must have been waiting outside on the lookout until Mom left. But he hadn't expected Yasmin to be home too.

"What are you doing here?" He wiped his face on his sleeve and pushed Yasmin out of the way.

"Someone had to look after your brother, didn't they?" she snapped, quickly grabbing the paper flowers off the table.

Jadran ran to the sofa where I was lying and jabbed his finger at Yasmin.

"She's not allowed to know about it," he whispered. "She has to leave!"

The corners of Yasmin's mouth twitched, but luckily she was getting used to Jadran. "I'll just go get those dwarfs off my door. Then you can take them with you tomorrow."

Jadran held his breath until Yasmin disappeared into the hallway to the bedrooms.

"Does Mom know you're here?" I asked.

"Don't you get it?" He pulled the cover off me. "You don't get it, do you?"

"What am I supposed to get?"

"They want to split us up! You're staying here and I have to go in the room next to Guillaume's. I've seen it myself!"

I took hold of Jadran's hands and tried to calm him by stroking his fingers. "I know, Giant. And I hate it too. Did Mika explain it to you?"

Jadran pulled away from me and went to the hall, where my wheelchair was. He grabbed the handles and frantically shook the wheelchair, trying to unfold it.

"You have to press down on the seat!" I shouted before he broke something.

Jadran banged the wheelchair into the sofa. "We're brothers. Brothers belong together. Get in!"

"Calm down. You're going way too fast. Anyway, I can't get into the chair by myself yet."

"Sorry, sorry. It's all my fault, isn't it?" First he pushed down the footrests and then he slid an arm under my legs, just like he'd seen Mika do. I didn't dare to protest.

"What exactly are you planning to do?" I asked when Jadran had safely deposited me in the wheelchair.

He picked up the gym bag that I'd taken to the hospital, which was still by the washing machine. I knew I should call Mom now. But I didn't do it.

"We have to be quick," he said, pushing the box of painkillers into the bag. "No one's allowed to see us!!"

Jadran stomped around, rummaging through stuff and packing the bag. I followed him in the wheelchair.

"Mom's going to go crazy when she hears that you've run away again." The muscles in my neck were twitching and I could feel the blood pounding in my head, but I did my best to talk as calmly as possible.

"You still don't get it! I'm not going away. *We're* going away. We have to stay together, Josh!" Then he spotted the pile of clothes that Mom was putting together for his new wardrobe. He took a pair of pants, socks, and a sweater and put them with the rest of the things in the gym bag.

I rolled toward him, put my hand on his wrist. "You're right. We belong together. But we can't just disappear. My leg's in a cast. And Mom . . ."

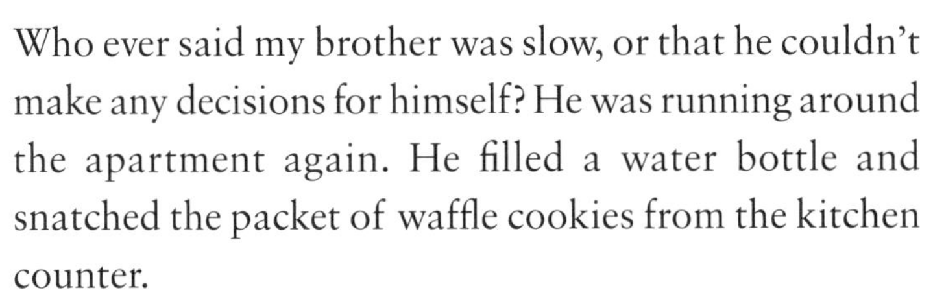

Who ever said my brother was slow, or that he couldn't make any decisions for himself? He was running around the apartment again. He filled a water bottle and snatched the packet of waffle cookies from the kitchen counter.

"Okay, Giant," I said when he finally stopped racing around. "Where do you want to go?"

Jadran looked toward the bedrooms, checking to see if Yasmin was secretly eavesdropping on us.

"We're taking Sprig home!" he hissed.

The tension slipped from my shoulders. "Is that it? You want us to take Sprig back together?"

I didn't think it was such a crazy idea. The cranes' lake wasn't too far, and he'd only just been there. We would go release Sprig together. We'd looked after him together and taught him how to fly again. It would be a nice farewell. A bunch of crepe-paper flowers didn't come close.

"But then we'll come straight back home, right?" I asked.

Jadran nodded and tossed my winter jacket onto my lap. Then he tried to put my walking boots on me.

"The cast is in the way," I said. "My foot won't fit anymore."

Jadran was unstoppable. And I didn't want to stop him anyway. I knew Mom wasn't going to like it though. But she'd messed things up herself this time by sending Jadran away. And I wanted her to know that!

Jadran walked out onto the balcony, gave Sprig something gross from his pocket, and picked him up. "Come on, Spriggie, you can come too."

Jadran pushed the crane against my stomach, grabbed the can of food, and hung the gym bag on one of the handles of the wheelchair. I clasped my hands around Sprig's wings so he couldn't bash me in the face. Then Jadran pushed me into the hallway.

"Wait a minute!" Yasmin came running after us with the rolled-up poster. She pulled the rubber band from her braid and slid it around the poster. "Where are you two off to so secretly?"

"Nowhere!" said Jadran. "We're not going anywhere, are we, Josh?"

Yasmin looked at me and then at the crane on my lap. Jadran towered menacingly above her. She tapped the gym bag with the poster.

"So what do you need that for?" she asked.

"Nothing!" Jadran chased Yasmin back.

She made a face. "Oh, so the two of you are off to have fun doing nothing nowhere, are you?"

Yasmin was not going to just shrug and give up. And lying to her would only complicate things even more.

"We're taking Sprig back," I confessed. "Jadran wants us to do it ourselves, just the two of us, before tomorrow."

Jadran glared at me. I'd blown our secret.

"I . . . am . . . staying . . . with . . . Josh," he stammered. "I don't want the room next to Guillaume's. I don't need my own bathroom."

Yasmin bit her lip. "Okay, do what you like. But you guys could have at least have come said . . . bye, huh?"

"Bye," repeated Jadran.

"And not a word to Mom or Murad," I hissed. "They have to find out for themselves. By the time they notice, we'll already be well on the way there."

Yasmin held up her hand and promised, as if she was swearing an oath. Jadran looked impressed. Then she pulled her phone out of her back pocket.

"Here, take this with you." She slipped the shiny

smartphone past Sprig's wings and into the inside pocket of my jacket. "For if your wheelchair breaks down. I'll use my dad's old phone until you get back." The way she looked at me with her coal-dark eyes made me feel kind of uncomfortable.

Jadran brushed past Yasmin.

"Oh yes, the code's the year we were born!" she called after us.

Then Jadran rolled me toward the elevator, full speed ahead.

The South
450

THE TRACTOR WAS PARKED WITH its rear wheels in the flower bed. The roses were snapped and the sidewalk was covered with crushed rose hips. The tractor was a small, old-fashioned, orange Fiat with a big wooden bucket attachment at the back for moving shovels and plants around. If you didn't know better, you'd think it belonged to the city gardening team.

But I did know better. The gardeners never parked their tractors in the plants like that. And there was an extra seat above the fenders on each side, so that two passengers could ride along safely.

Passengers from the Space.

"You stole the tractor!" I shouted.

"Didn't steal it." Jadran swung the gym bag into the bucket. There were still a few potatoes and a trowel in it.

"Do you mean we're going to drive in that?" I asked.

"You can sit in Mika's seat," he said, like it was a huge honor.

He put Sprig on a fender, took me in his arms, and lifted me onto the plastic seat. It had a sturdy backrest, and luckily there was a belt to strap me in. It was a really tight fit though. My cast was jammed up against the driver's seat. I had to be careful not to accidentally step on one of the pedals.

Sprig was clearly not impressed. He kept pattering back and forth and getting ready to jump down.

Jadran stood up again, took hold of the crane, and pressed him against my chest. "Hold on tightly to him!"

He managed to fold up the wheelchair surprisingly quickly. He pushed the footrests aside, lifted the seat, and slid it into the bucket. Then he climbed behind the steering wheel and stuck the key in the ignition. He put his foot on a pedal and turned the starter. The tractor rumbled to life. A stinky cloud of smoke rose up. We jolted backward, even deeper into the flowerbed. And then the tractor came to a stop.

"Sorry." Jadran flapped the smoke away and rattled the gearshift. The engine roared. Lumps of mud flew all around.

Then we rumbled onto the street.

We drove past the apartment block. I didn't dare to look up. Maybe Rafaela was watching us. Or maybe Yasmin was waving us off, after first having let Mom know what we were up to. Jadran had his eyes firmly fixed on the asphalt too. At a snail's pace, we rolled past the parked cars.

A girl on a moped overtook us and looked back like she'd never seen a tractor before. But she wasn't looking at the tractor, or at Sprig, or at my leg in its cast. She was looking at Jadran. At the way he was bent over the steering wheel, with his eyes squeezed into slits, and the tip of his tongue poking out of his mouth.

A van was coming our way.

"Keep to the right, Giant!"

Jadran gave the steering wheel a tug. The wheels grated against the curb. We bounced back and forth. I struggled to keep Sprig and myself on board.

Cars honked their horns. A man raised his fist. Jadran bit his tongue. He gripped the steering wheel until his knuckles turned white.

Screwing up his face in concentration, he pushed down on the gas pedal.

His driving was getting better. We went past the high school where I'd be going next year, a huge rust-brown building without any drawings or decorations on the windows. I caught a glimpse of us reflected in the glass: Jadran at the steering wheel with his look of determination. Me with my cast and a crane on my lap. The wheelchair in the bucket. It was no wonder everyone was giving us such strange looks.

We drove past the movie theater and the drugstore where Rafaela worked. We bumped over the median strip, followed a footpath, and took a shortcut across the pedestrian zone by the library.

I could see that Jadran wasn't taking the shortest route to the cranes' lake. That would have meant taking the ring road and then going into the woods after the industrial park. He'd been there just a couple days ago, so he knew the way, but he seemed to have come up with a different route. His own secret route for tractors.

We followed a network of interweaving streets and squares. I didn't even recognize some of the places, but Jadran took every fork and every roundabout without any hesitation.

It was market day in the Southside. There were stalls everywhere and stallholders shouting at the top of their voices. The scent of cut flowers and spices mingled with fried sausage and Turkish bread. The people here didn't seem so surprised to see the tractor. Maybe they thought Jadran was a farm boy bringing fresh produce from the field—and that I was perched up there with some kind of weird-looking chicken.

The river lay behind the market square. Jadran drove up to the water and parked neatly between the white lines on the concrete. Then he turned off the engine.

"Why are you stopping, Giant?"

Jadran looked at the clouds hanging above the river like flying ships.

"I don't know the rest of the way," he said.

"I'll help you. The lake's in that direction." I pointed back the way we'd come and then right and into the woods.

He didn't even look.

"South," he mumbled. "The south is in Spain."

I looked for the sun so I could show him which direction the south was in. But there were too many clouds.

"And this is the Southside, isn't it? Sometimes we buy vegetables here with Mika. And then we make goulash like her grandma does."

I nodded. "But we're not going to buy anything now. We have to keep going with Sprig."

Jadran beamed and gave the crane a stroke.

Sprig let the soccer referee's whistle in his throat blow. *Spririririree*.

"Just like in the video," said Jadran.

"With that hang glider, you mean?"

"With the tractor, stupid. We're taking Sprig to Spain."

I was too surprised to say anything. Jadran didn't want to go back to the lake at all. *We're taking Sprig home*, he'd said, *to his family*. But he meant their vacation home in the south!

I slapped the tractor with both hands. It sounded like a broken gong.

"We can't go to Spain," I said. "Spain's way too far."

"We'll drive there on the tractor."

I shook my head. "Come on, Giant, let's go home."

"I'm not allowed to go home." Jadran's face looked so sad. "I have to go to the room next to Guillaume's. But you don't. You're staying with Mom."

I thought of my room. The two mattresses next to each other. How good it felt to lie with my head on Jadran's warm tummy.

"You really don't want to go, do you?" I said.

Jadran gazed across to the other side of the river again. As if Spain was waiting for us out there in the grass somewhere.

For a few minutes, nothing happened. A bunch of ducks put their heads under the water, so that only their fluffy butts were visible. The market people screamed themselves hoarse.

"There!" Jadran suddenly shouted.

Far above the city, a group of wild geese flew over. They chattered loudly with every beat of their wings and flew away over the residential neighborhoods across the river. Jadran hurried back to the tractor and turned on the engine.

"We have to follow them," he said, petting Sprig. "They're flying south too."

"That's ridiculous, Giant!" I shouted above the din. "There's no way we're driving all that way!"

But I couldn't stop him. And I didn't really want to stop him now. Everything Jadran had said to me back at the apartment was still echoing around inside my head: *We're brothers. Brothers always stay together. I want to be with you, Josh*. Mika was planning to split us up. And Mom agreed. I couldn't let it happen—we had to get away! This was our chance to escape.

The tractor rumbled and spluttered. A grey cloud of smoke drifted toward the market stalls.

"Wait for us!" whooped Jadran, looking up at the sky.

And he juddered off down the street again, following the geese.

THE SOUTH IS ALWAYS THERE. Sometimes it's on your left, sometimes on the right or straight ahead. But whichever way you go, it's only a step away. You just have to be able to see it.

For Jadran, the south was beyond the wind turbines. That's where the geese had disappeared from sight. So that's where we were heading on the tractor, as quickly as we could.

It was a ridiculous plan, a plan that only Jadran could have come up with. But the more I thought about it, the more exciting it seemed! We were going on the tractor to take Sprig to the cranes' winter resting place. Without parents, he'd never be able to find the way.

We weren't just any old brothers. We were crane brothers. And we were taking Sprig to the only place he belonged: with his family.

Beyond the river, residential neighborhoods gave way to a patchwork of meadows and fields. The wind turbines towered high above them. Their blades seemed to turn to the rhythm of the tractor wheels.

Jadran drove along the bike path. Obviously that wasn't allowed, but it was safer because the trucks were racing past at breakneck speed. The cyclists weren't too happy about it though. And it didn't help that Jadran squeezed his eyes shut every time a bike came too close.

"Out of the way, Giant!" I yelled.

The cyclist rang his bell. Jadran almost drove into the roadside.

At a roundabout, we turned onto a narrow farm road that led to the wind turbines in the distance.

"We need a compass," I said.

"What's a compass?" asked Jadran.

"One of those round things with a needle that lets you work out the wind direction."

Jadran nodded like he understood. "Those wind turbines are turning in the direction of the wind."

"That's true. But a compass always shows which way is north and south, even if the wind is blowing from the other direction. It doesn't actually have anything to do with the wind. It's magnetism or something, I think."

Jadran grinned. "Mika's a magnet."

"Huh?"

"That's what Mom said. I always stick to Mika. That's because she's a magnet."

The road became bumpier. My butt cheeks were sore.

"We don't need a compass," said Jadran. "The south is in Spain. Even when the wind's not blowing."

"Yes," I said. "For us it is. But it doesn't stop after Spain, because that's where North Africa is."

Jadran tapped his forehead, like I'd just said something really dumb. "*South* Africa, you mean!"

"And then if you keep on going, you end up at the penguins," I said.

"Penguins are cool." Jadran flapped his hands like two stumpy little wings.

"Hold the steering wheel, Giant!"

The bells in a far-off church tower rang four times. In half an hour, Mom would go fetch Jadran from the Space and find that he was missing. And that me and my broken leg were gone too. I didn't dare to think about what a shock she'd have this time.

Sprig was getting more and more restless. He kept trying to stand up. Toenails were poking through my pants and scratching the cast. He raised his wings and sharpened his beak on the back of the passenger seat.

"Stop a second," I said. "I can't hold onto Sprig."

Even before the tractor stopped, Sprig flew down to the ground.

We looked south. Jadran was looking at the south with the wind turbines. And I was looking at the south beyond.

"It could be, like, more than a thousand miles," I said. "To the cranes."

"Wow," said Jadran, even though he had no idea how far that actually was.

"The tractor goes a maximum of only fifteen miles an hour. So if we drive for ten hours a day, when will we get there?" It was like a math problem at school. "Ten times fifteen. That makes one hundred fifty."

Jadran nodded.

"So how many days do we have to drive?" I asked.

His brain was creaking. I held up my fingers to help him.

". . . five, six, seven?" he counted.

"Almost a week then, if we don't get lost." I tried to smile, but my mouth had seized up. It was Sunday tomorrow. And Monday I had to go to school.

Jadran beamed like he'd come up with the answer himself.

"A week's over in no time!" he shouted.

"I CAN DO SOMETHING," SAID JADRAN.

"What's that?"

"Whistle on my elbow." He bent his arm and pressed his mouth to the inside of his elbow. A shrill, high-pitched note sounded, like a singing kettle.

"Cool," I said.

Jadran whistled as loud as he could. The kettle was about to boil over.

"You see!" he said with a red face. "I can do something, huh? Something no one else can do!"

"We have to keep going, Giant," I said. "If someone sees us here, we can forget about it. They'll pick us up and send us straight back."

"Sprig!" shouted Jadran, spreading his arms like a big bird net. "Come on!"

But Sprig didn't want to sit on my lap. Not for a fresh worm. And not for a bit of waffle. He scrabbled around with his feet among the fall flowers until the earth beneath them was bare, pecking wildly at anything that moved. He seemed to have completely forgotten about Jadran and me.

There was nothing I could do. Dumb leg. If I leaned forward too far, I'd slide off the tractor.

So I said, "Start the engine."

"We're not going to leave him behind, are we?"

"We'll see if he follows us."

Jadran stomped my way again. His eyes were shining.

"Just like that plane, huh?" he said. "Like that hang glider. And I'm the pilot!"

Sprig pretended not to hear the roar of the engine. He didn't look up until Jadran drove the tractor back onto the road. He rubbed the sand off his beak one last time and sprinted after us.

Ie! Ieuw! That was probably crane language for "Stop! Stop!"

But Jadran didn't stop. He looked back at the running bird and kept stepping harder on the gas.

"A bit faster, pilot!"

Sprig was almost stumbling over his long stilts. He dashed and leaped. Then he opened up his wings and took off. Low above the ground, he flapped after the tractor. With a few steady beats of his wings, he was over our heads. And he just kept floating there, with his enormous shadow on the asphalt.

Jadran cheered. "He's doing it! That's what I said, didn't I? I always say everything, don't I?"

Iee! Iee! went Sprig.

"Yes, Giant," I said with a smile. "You always say everything."

We drove until our butts were blue from all the bumping. Sprig would fly above us for a while and then disappear from sight. But he always came back to the tractor.

After the wind turbines, we zigzagged across the landscape, heading in the direction we thought was south. We didn't have a route worked out, and maybe that was why no one was on our heels yet. Sometimes we went off the road for a bit and drove across a field. Or we chose a track through the woods where you couldn't go with an ordinary car.

We stopped near a grove of trees on the edge of a small creek. Jadran opened up the wheelchair and helped me into it. Then he disappeared into the blackberry bushes with a packet of tissues.

I ate a waffle cookie and Jadran gobbled down the rest of the packet. The water bottle was almost empty too.

"I'll fill it in the creek," said Jadran.

"No, don't do that!" I said. "Do you want to get poisoned?"

But he was already charging off with the bottle in his hand. I hurried after him in the wheelchair.

People often came here to picnic. There was a clearing on the banks of the creek, where you could easily get down to the water. Among the trees lay plastic bags, beer cans, and even more tissues.

Someone had tied a rope and a car tire to the branch of a willow tree. Jadran stormed toward it. He took a running start, grabbed the rope, and pulled up his legs.

"Yee-haaaw!" He swung wildly across the creek.

The branch creaked with every swing, but Jadran just stuck out his legs even more, pushing himself higher and higher.

"What about me?" I yelled from my wheelchair.

"I'll come get you, brother!" shouted Jadran. "We'll stay together, huh? We'll always stay together!"

He whirled back my way and dropped onto the ground. I rolled the chair toward him and pulled myself up on the rope with all my might. Dr. Mbasa's exercises came in handy now.

Jadran stood behind me and in front of me and around me so that I couldn't fall. He pushed my leg with the plaster cast onto the car tire. I clung on as tightly as I could. Everything hurt, and the stitches pulled tight when I tensed my muscles, but I did it anyway.

Jadran took hold of the rope, with me between his arms. He pushed off again and pulled his feet up. We swung back and forth. The bottom of Jadran's jacket dragged through the mud. The branch bent worryingly, and the dark water flowed past beneath us. It could have been the runoff from the sewer. But for Jadran, it was a stream in paradise. A laugh bubbled up inside him, a laugh I hadn't heard for a long time. A real, wild, boy's laugh.

I said, "On three, we both let go."

We went back and forth again.

"One, two, and . . ."

Jadran went flying onto the ground, landing on his cheek with his arms folded behind his back. I flopped onto his belly, rolled, and lay there on my side to keep my plaster cast dry.

For a second, we both held our breath together.

"You okay, Giant?"

Jadran burst out laughing. "Now I can never go to the Space! I have to stay here with you forever!"

WE LAY AMONG THE TREES and pretended we were both invisible. Jadran was an expert at it.

"Where are you?" I said. "You were lying there just a second ago and now you're gone!"

"Helloo!" he shouted.

I turned my head in every direction, pretending not to see him.

"At the top of the tree!" Jadran stood up to make himself look bigger.

"How do you do that?" I lifted my chin and searched the branches. "Stop teasing me! Come on out and show yourself!"

"Here," he whispered, closer now. "Yoo-hoo!"

I grabbed his foot and gave it a tug.

"Hey, what's going on?" he shouted. "My foot's stuck on something. Help!"

Jadran fell onto his knees. I threw my arm around his neck and looked right at him.

“Ah, so there you are!” I said with a laugh.

But Jadran just went on playing and stayed invisible until it was time to leave.

It was hard work getting me back across the creek, but we did it. I asked Jadran to look under the trees for the longest branch he could find. He stretched out with the branch to grab the rope. He staggered and almost fell into the water, but he managed to pull the car tire to our side. We scrubbed the dirt off our clothes with the towel that Jadran had stuffed in the gym bag before we left. Jadran put on dry socks. A chunk crumbled off the bottom of my cast.

Soon it started to get dark and the tractor’s headlights cast a thin, yellowish glow ahead of us. Sprig was in his element. He flew low over the fields and whistled at the setting sun. I hoped he would trumpet as beautifully as the adult cranes, but he didn’t get more than that shrill squeaking out of his beak.

“We have to find a place to sleep,” I said.

“I’m not tired yet,” mumbled Jadran.

“In the dark we can’t see which way south is.”

We were standing in a hilly landscape, with small farms dotted among orchards. There were lights on in some of the buildings.

“I’ll go ask,” said Jadran.

"What?"

"If they have a room. With two mattresses next to each other."

"Are you serious? They'll call Mom."

Jadran turned onto a long lane. A sheepdog barked hoarsely when it saw the tractor. The lane led to a neglected-looking village. In the middle was a village square with a rickety kiosk and a line of pruned trees. Smoke curled from a chimney. And, along with the smoke, a strong scent of food came our way.

Jadran abruptly parked the tractor on the roadside. He licked his lips.

"If you want something, you have to ask for it. That's what Mika says."

"Don't do it, Jadran. Stay there."

But he jumped down and walked across the square to the house the delicious smell was coming from. In the light of the streetlamps, he didn't look like a boy anymore, but a grown man. A hunched-up man who had come to beg for some food.

The door opened a crack. A woman in a sweat suit put her head out. She was wearing dark glasses, and her grey hair was gleaming as if she'd just taken a shower.

I couldn't hear what Jadran said, but she didn't close the door and she didn't chase him away.

Jadran was a born charmer, as I knew only too well. Rafaela, Mika the magnet, and Mom herself: with a simple smile, he won them all over.

"It's because he can see right through you," said Mom when I asked her why that was. "Jadran doesn't look at the outside. He makes people feel that he sees them as they really are."

The woman went back inside. Jadran turned and gave me a thumbs up.

A little later, the woman returned with not one but two steaming plastic containers. Jadran must have thanked her a hundred times. She smiled awkwardly, as if she wasn't entirely sure she'd done the right thing.

Jadran hurried back to the tractor with the containers.

They had roast potatoes in them. And thick, creamy gravy.

"How did you manage that?" I asked.

"Oh, you know," he said, like he went out begging every day. "I just said her food smelled real good."

His eyes were twinkling.

We ate every last bit of the food and then drove on into the darkness. It was a bright night with a clear sky.

The stars and planets shone much more brightly here than above our apartment block in the city. Sprig landed on the tractor and even he sat staring up at the sky with an open beak.

A little way past the village, we came to a railroad crossing. The barriers had been removed, and it was clear that no trains had passed this way for years. On the other side of the railroad tracks, there was a wooden construction trailer. The paint was peeling and one of the windows was broken. The rusty logo of the railroad company hung above the door.

"That's it," I said. "Our hotel for tonight."

Jadran shook his head, but he still steered the tractor in that direction without a murmur. Beyond the crossing, he drove up the concrete track to a spot behind the trailer. So no one would really notice the tractor from the street.

"Go check if the door's locked," I said.

Jadran turned off the engine and slid down the fender. He climbed the steps, pressed down the door handle, and gave the door a thump.

"Boom!" he shouted as the door grated open. "Boom! Boom!"

Then I heard a beep. Startled, Sprig flapped off my lap. It was Yasmin's phone, vibrating against my chest.

I took it out of my inside pocket and tapped in the code. The screen lit up.

Everything OK? They're looking for you at the lake. X. Yaz.

It wasn't just the telephone trembling—it was my whole body.

That was when I *really* realized what we were doing. Up until that point it had seemed more like a game: the crane, the tractor, running away to the south. It was exciting, and we were doing what we felt like doing.

But Yasmin's message wasn't a game. We'd actually run away. Everyone was looking for us.

I gave the telephone to Jadran. He studied the message carefully, letter by letter.

"There's an X too many," he said.

SLEEPING IS THE SHORTEST WAY through the night. At least it is if you don't get lost.

I dreamed about birds. Blue wings that had grown on my back. I stood on the balcony and heard the feathers rustling. A cloud of birds hung above the apartment block. They were all chirping at once.

Go on, Josh, jump and let the wind take you!

And then they flew in circles, skimming the building.

Don't be afraid, Josh! Flying's the best thing in the world!

They took hold of me, and thousands of beaks lifted me up. They carried me with them, higher and higher above the city.

Oh, Josh, you have the most beautiful wings of all of us.

If you really want to do something, then you can!

And then they let go of me, all those beaks at once.

For one moment, I was plummeting down. For that one terrible moment, I thought I'd be smashed to pieces.

But then the blue wings swept open—and off I flew.

Jadran jolted me awake when he turned to lie on his other side. Which he did every ten minutes. His elbows banged against the floorboards, and his knees jabbed me in the back.

But then how could you sleep well on a bare floor, with nothing but a blanket to protect you from the cold and a gym bag for a pillow? There were cracks everywhere, the shutters rattled, and the whole trailer rocked with the wind. It was making me seasick. And it was making Jadran cough. He was coughing so hard that it seemed like trains were thundering along the abandoned railroad tracks again.

At six o'clock, when a nearby donkey began to bray, we decided we'd had enough. Only Sprig still had his head buried deep in his feathers.

"Let's go," muttered Jadran, stuffing everything back into the gym bag.

"I need to go to the bathroom first," I said.

I thought about the hospital, how a nurse had to help me onto the toilet and how awkward it had been.

But Jadran had no problem with it. He helped me like a real nurse. Very carefully, he led me down the steps of the trailer. He looked away at the right moment and then held out the tissues.

I took out the telephone again and reread Yasmin's message. The less she knows about us, the better, I thought. She'd sworn an oath, but would she be able to keep her mouth shut? I still couldn't resist writing something back though. As long as I kept it vague enough, it couldn't do any harm, could it?

With numb fingers, I typed:

`Everything's okay. No need for mom to worry.`

Without an X.

Sprig sat drowsily on my lap. Jadran turned right, even though I had no idea if that was the right direction. There wasn't even a line of sun on the horizon yet. A light was on behind the curtain in one house, but otherwise everything was dark. Jadran seemed to have made up his mind though.

"How do you know for certain that we need to go that way?"

"Look, Josh. Don't you see?" Jadran held up his hand and pointed at the dark roof of one of the houses. "Those shiny things. They're sun panels, right?"

"Um, yes."

"Well then."

"Well then what?" I was getting irritable.

"Sun panels point at the sun. Otherwise they're not sun panels."

Then I saw what he meant. All the solar panels were facing more or less in the same direction. Jadran was right. They were like signposts pointing to the sun, even when it was nowhere to be seen.

"You're a genius!" I shouted.

And Jadran kept repeating that for ages. "Did you hear that, Sprig? I'm a genius! And geniuses always go the right way. Don't they, Josh? Geniuses never get lost."

It was still really chilly outside. I pushed Sprig out of the way and pulled the blanket up over my chin. Jadran wasn't bothered by the cold. He clenched one hand on the steering wheel and the other around the gearshift. He straightened his back and looked like he'd never done anything but carry cranes and injured brothers around on a tractor.

The tension after Yasmin and Murad arrived, the accident and the move to the Space—it all seemed so far away.

I hadn't seen my brother this content in a long time.

So cheerful and self-confident.

Until I started talking about Dad.

WE WERE DRIVING THROUGH OPEN countryside, with stubbly fields and endless hedges. I gave Sprig some of the food we'd brought. He greedily pecked the grains of corn from my hand. Jadran sat humming to himself. There was a bunch of dark fuzz on his top lip.

"Do you ever think about him?" I asked.

Jadran looked around. "About who?"

"Dad."

At home I never dared ask about him. Mom didn't like it. She was afraid it would upset Jadran. But here, with my brother humming away so blissfully, I did dare.

"Why? Dad's gone."

"Yes, of course. That's the point."

I hardly remembered anything about Dad myself. I couldn't—Dad had left before I could really talk. The first couple of years he'd sometimes called from Russia or sent a postcard from some even more remote country. But then it stopped. Almost all the images I had of him were secondhand. They came from photos I found among the junk in the basement, a folder of newspaper clippings about his performances with Mom, the things that she or Jadran told me.

Jadran shook Dad out of his head again.

"It's my fault," he said. "Everything's always my fault, isn't it?"

"Stop it, Giant. Why don't you tell me something nice about back then instead? I was tiny when he left, but you must still remember stuff."

"I don't remember anything."

"Those wings of Mom's, for example. She used them in a musical with Dad. And you loved their performances, didn't you?"

Jadran forgot to step on the gas. We slowly rolled until the tractor came to a stop. I should never have mentioned Dad.

"*The Blue Angel*," he murmured. "Dad gave me some colored pencils. Half of the tips were broken. I had to sit at the back of the room. But I didn't color. I watched."

"And what did you see?"

"They sang to each other. Mom was wearing those wings, and Dad had a long coat and a big moustache."

"Dad with a moustache? That sounds funny."

"Yuck! They started kissing in front of the whole room."

"Oh, so they still loved each other?"

Jadran made a sour face, like he'd just bitten into something really gross.

Then he slammed his foot on the pedal again.

It made Sprig jump. He hopped onto the back of the seat, flapped his wings, and took off. He flew an extra circle when we went too slowly, turned with us whenever we went around a bend, and cried out shrilly when he lost sight of us among the trees.

"I'm hungry," grumbled Jadran as we drove into yet another village. "Breakfast's always at half past seven. Is it half past seven yet, Josh? We can't have breakfast too late."

The village was nothing more than a long line of houses. There was no sign of a store. But in the middle of the village street there was a vending machine with loaves of bread inside.

"Got any change?" I asked.

Jadran dug around in his jacket. Mom sometimes gave him some pocket money, and he'd fished the smallest coins out of the fountain. They jingled in his hand. He put them into the slot, one by one, but the machine didn't accept the five-cent pieces. Time after time, they rolled into the tray at the bottom. And, every time, Jadran pushed them back in.

"It doesn't like them!" He gave the side of the machine such a thump that it made the glass shake. "I want some bread!"

On the other side of the street, there was a small garage where they repaired mopeds and lawnmowers. The door opened. A man in stained overalls came out to take a look.

"What's going on here?"

"I'm hungry! I want some bread, but I can't get it!"

"Shh," I said. "Stop using the copper coins. It'll work with the ten and twenty cents."

But Jadran just put all the five-cent pieces in again. They rattled straight through the machine.

Boom! He banged his forehead against the glass.

Boom! "Bread!" *Boom!*

I knew Jadran wasn't that upset because of the bread. Dad was still racing around inside his head.

The mechanic was on the sidewalk in front of the garage by then. He had the eyebrows of a yeti. All the hair from his scalp seemed to have slid down to the spot over his eyes.

"Go on, Giant. Just use the gold coins." I wanted to help him, but I was glued to the tractor seat because of that miserable plaster cast.

The man shambled across the street. Sprig hurried to the roof of a shed. Frightened, Jadran dropped the copper coins. They clinked onto the concrete. I really didn't want him going crazy now.

"Quick!" I shouted. "Let's get out of here." I slid forward a little and put my good leg on the step. Clasping one hand on the tractor, I pushed myself up with the other.

"I haven't seen you two around here before." The mechanic wiped his hands on his overalls.

"We wanted to buy some bread," I replied. "But the machine wasn't working and my brother . . ."

"Thought he'd just give it a bash?" said the man. If the yeti existed, it'd probably sound just as grumpy.

Jadran fell onto his knees to pick up the coins. His whole body was shaking.

"Bread," he mumbled. "I just want some bread."

"Keep breathing," I whispered. "The man's not going to hurt you. Breathe in deep, and then breathe out slowly."

I tried to get closer to him. I put my weight on my hands and moved my foot lower. But my plaster cast got stuck behind the gearshift. And I slipped.

"Giant, I—"

Before Jadran could do anything, I fell off the tractor.

The man stared in amazement at my brother and then at me, lying there on the road with my leg in the air. Then he reached out his hairy arm to help me up.

But he wasn't taking Jadran into account. Jadran scrambled to his feet, stuck out his chin, and stood right in front of me. His big hands waved menacingly above the man.

"Leave him alone!" he barked. "Josh is my brother."

The mechanic took a step back and wiped the beads of sweat from his forehead.

"Sorry, guys," he said, now in a completely different tone. "I just thought . . ."

"Brothers always stay together!" Jadran took me in his arms and carefully lifted me back up onto the tractor.

While the stunned man watched, Jadran picked up the last of the money off the ground.

"The gold coins," I said again. "Just use the gold coins."

Jadran tried one more time. The door of the machine finally clicked open and he pulled out a loaf. He shoved half a slice of bread into his mouth and climbed back up behind the steering wheel.

Then he made the engine roar louder than ever before.

PAST THE VILLAGE WE CAME onto a long, broad road. On both sides there were low fruit trees covered with nets. I'd scraped my arm when I fell, and I couldn't manage to sit there calmly. What if that yeti called the police?

Jadran seemed to have forgotten the man already. He was humming louder and louder. And soon, with his lips covered in breadcrumbs, he was singing some oldie song about falling in love again.

I recognized the song. Jadran often hummed it. But never when Mom was around. It made her twitchy.

I leaned forward as far as I could.

"Is that from *The Blue Angel*?" I called above the drone of the engine.

Jadran held the steering wheel with one hand and rummaged around in the bag of bread with the other.

"Mom sang it at a bar," he said. "And then Dad

came to watch her. But she didn't like that. She pushed him away, but he kept coming back with his gross moustache."

"Do you mean at the theater?" I asked. "And the bar was the set?"

Jadran nodded. "The whole room clapped. And after, they pulled Mom up with the blue wings on."

I slid forward a bit more so that I didn't miss anything. A pain shot through my leg. "Was she flying?"

"She was hanging on a rope above the stage. I saw it myself. She went right up to the ceiling. At the end, she was gone."

"And what about Dad?"

"He was lying dead on the ground."

"Dad's not dead. He's gone, but he's not dead."

"On the stage, idiot."

"Okay, genius."

I took a piece of bread from the bag too. I picked off some crumbs, squashed them into little balls, and put them on my tongue like pieces of candy.

Jadran wasn't humming anymore. He was staring straight ahead.

"They argued in the car," he said.

"On the way home, you mean?"

"They were yelling at each other. But yelling's not allowed, is it?"

All I had left was a crust. A thin, brown crust with a hole in the middle. I tried to make shapes out of it: a square, an egg, a bird.

A big, hollowed-out heart.

Jadran straightened his back and lowered his voice.

"It can't go on like this!" he suddenly shouted.

Sprig jumped.

"Huh? You talking to me?" I asked.

"It's now or never, Margot."

"Oh, you mean Mom?"

Jadran didn't reply. He was in the back seat of Mom and Dad's car again, and he was completely absorbed in their conversation.

"We can't stop now," he said in Dad's voice. "We have the opportunity to perform in Russia. Don't you get it? You still don't get it, do you?"

Jadran raised his eyebrows like Mom sometimes did and spoke like a young woman. "Come on, Max. Jadran can't take it anymore. The traveling, all the people. It's not good for him. As you're well aware."

Jadran was performing a play. That was how it seemed. He was using complicated sentences and words he didn't entirely understand. But this wasn't a play. It was a real fight between Mom and Dad. And it was fixed in his memory forever.

"It's our dream, Margot," said Dad. "We'll conquer the world. And now we're getting to perform in Russia—just imagine!"

"This is no life for a child like him," replied Mom. "And with little Josh too . . ."

"Jadran doesn't have to come. There are special places for boys like him. Better places than a theater or a hotel. And when we're on vacation . . ."

"He's your son! You can't just leave him behind!"

Jadran stepped on the brake. The tractor jerked to a stop. Sprig flew on a bit and then came back in a wide curve and perched in a nearby tree.

"So you're quitting?" Jadran's voice sounded even deeper than before.

He stuck his chin in the air and blew out with a big sigh.

"Don't force me to choose, Max," said Mom.

Sprig flew down from the tree and hopped over to Jadran, who was now sitting with his back against one of the wheels of the tractor. I wished I could hug his head to my chest and comfort him, but I was stuck there in the seat. Sprig tugged Jadran's laces loose with his beak. Jadran just let him.

"Is that how it happened?" I asked. "Is that when Mom and Dad split up?"

Jadran looked up to where I was sitting. The clouds were reflected in his eyes.

"It's all my fault, isn't it?" he whispered. "Everything's always my fault."

Radio Tower

Where are you guys?! X. Yas.

-Can't tell you anything. J.

They sent out a missing person alert. Your photo looks really dumb. Bad hair day!

-How's mom doing?

She wants them to drag the lake.

-What?!

With divers and everything. She's scared you guys drove that dumb tractor into it.

-Tell her we're not in the lake.

Then where are you?

-Duh.

Go on, I'm kind of like your sister now.

-You think?

By the way, that's my phone! X.

Jadran didn't want to hear what Yasmin had written. He was trying to strike up a conversation with Sprig, who was tidying up his feathers on the seat on the other fender.

"We'll find them," he said. "Your family's waiting for you. They're collecting beetles for you."

Sprig pecked at the needle that indicated the speed. His beak tapped the glass.

"Hey, it's not a worm, Sprig," laughed Jadran. "It says fifteen. That's how fast we're going."

Then Sprig took off, as if he wanted to show that he could go much faster. He flapped a bit ahead of the tractor, drifted on a gust of wind, and then came back and flew directly above us. His flight feathers swished. His belly feathers were smooth. It was no effort at all for Sprig to stay in the air now.

Being able to breathe like a bird—that'd be so amazing! With air sacs in your body and cavities in your bones, so the oxygen could flow all the way from your chest to the tips of your wings. And to feel yourself getting lighter and lighter with every breath, so light that your body slowly rose.

Full and free, into the clouds.

Jadran was making funny faces. He put two fingers up his nose and pushed down the corners of his eyes. It looked scary, but I laughed anyway. He was finally cheerful again.

"Have you heard that joke about Winnie the Pooh?" he asked.

"No," I lied.

Jadran put on a voice like a schoolteacher. "How are Winnie the Pooh and Jadran the Giant the same?"

"Jadran the Giant . . . ? Oh, I know," I answered, as I was supposed to. "They share the same middle name, huh?"

"No, no, no, I got you!" Jadran doubled up. "You're wrong! They're both really fond of honey candies!"

He'd already told that joke a hundred times. But we still roared with laughter.

We drove on until midday and parked the tractor in the shelter of a sunken road. We went and lay down in some grass higher up on the bank and ate some bread. The ground was damp, but the fall sunshine made up for a lot.

Sprig fluffed up his feathers, stuck his beak under his wing, and stood napping on one leg. Jadran dozed off too. I wasn't sleepy. I could really feel the stabbing pain in my leg now, and my skin burning under the plaster.

For a while, nothing happened.

Leaves rustled. Shapeless clouds drifted past.

Then a car slowed down in the sunken road. A red Volvo with a long trunk pulled up behind our tractor. The sound of the door opening startled Jadran awake.

"Quiet, Giant," I whispered before he could say anything.

Footsteps crunched on the gravel. Jadran pressed himself even deeper into the grass.

All I could see was the top of a black hat. And an army jacket with a fake-fur collar. I tried to breathe as calmly as possible. Maybe the driver had just gotten out to make a call. To smoke a cigarette. To pee.

Jadran's fingers reached for my hand.

"Follow my breath, Giant," I whispered. "In and out. We're not here right now."

Sprig was there though. He stuck his beak in the air and sounded his alarm.

Ee eeoo! With two big flaps of his wings, he took off.

The driver stood still and pushed up his hat, as if he wanted to make sure that it really was a crane. Then he turned around, wiped the dirt off his shoes onto the grass, and walked back to the car.

Why didn't he come any closer? There was an empty wheelchair at the side of the road. With stickers of flames on the side! So you'd go see if someone was in trouble, wouldn't you?

Footsteps crunched on the stones. The car door slammed shut. The engine started.

Jadran's fingers rasped over my skin.

WE WAITED UNTIL THE VOLVO had disappeared around the bend. Sprig hung high above us. As soon as the tractor started moving, he flapped away. This time we had to follow him—that was how it seemed. And he was in a real hurry. Jadran set off in pursuit. The tractor left a trail of mud on the asphalt.

"Wait for us, Sprig," shouted Jadran. "You're flying more than fifteen miles an hour!"

Sprig wasn't just flying too fast. I didn't think he had any clue which direction to fly in either. We blasted our way through blackberry bushes. He flew across a freshly plowed field. We almost got stuck in the deep tracks of a much bigger tractor.

And when we finally caught up with him, Sprig calmly flew off in the opposite direction.

Ahead of us was a residential neighborhood with pretty flower beds and a sports field.

"Can't we go around it?" I asked. There were people walking everywhere and children playing. "A bit of a detour won't hurt."

But Jadran didn't want to hear about detours. For him, everything was always straight ahead.

Yasmin had written that they were looking for us. Maybe they'd put up posters in the meantime and were handing out leaflets.

"Don't stare at people like that, Giant," I said. "And wipe that spit off your chin. We don't want anyone to recognize us. Got it?"

A bunch of kids in scouting uniforms were already shouting: "Did you see that? It's a stork!"

I wanted the ground to swallow me up. Jadran twisted his mouth into a weird grimace and grinned at the people walking by. He actually seemed to be enjoying all the attention.

"They think we're cool," he said. "The supercool crane brothers. That's us, huh?"

Jadran ignored a traffic sign and almost ended up in a strip of fresh concrete. I just managed to get him to turn in time. A little farther on, a police car was parked by a roundabout. A policewoman was talking sternly to a motorcyclist. If she looked around right now . . .

"Go right!" I shouted.

Jadran tugged the wheel left, then corrected his mistake and swerved into the street I was pointing at. "What now?"

On the sidewalk, a lady stood chatting away to her dachshund. Two men with a baby stroller were coming from the other direction.

We had to get out of there as quickly as possible.

One neighborhood turned into the next. Some of them had apartment blocks just like ours. You didn't see any solar panels here, just satellite dishes like grey foghorns on the balconies. I directed Jadran past a park where some teenagers were skateboarding. They'd made a ramp out of a broken billboard and were jumping over it as high as they could.

For a moment, I wanted to join in. To do ordinary things with ordinary boys like me. And not to have to look after my brother all the time. But I couldn't skateboard. My leg was broken in three places. I could barely go to the bathroom on my own.

We were only just past the park when the engine cut out. The tractor sputtered and stopped. Jadran turned the key and put his foot on the gas. The tractor lurched forward a bit but it was still rattling away.

"Get off the road," I said.

My brother turned the steering wheel and slowly maneuvered the tractor to the side. The muffler blew a grey cloud into the air, and that was it.

"It's not working. It's broken!" Jadran bashed the steering wheel.

"When did you last fill it up?" I asked.

Jadran frowned. "I've never filled it up!"

"Then the tank's probably empty."

Jadran pointed at the fuel gauge on the dashboard: "Half full."

"Maybe the meter's broken?"

Jadran clapped his hands together. "Everything's broken at the Space!"

"Everything? What do you mean?"

"Sarah-with-an-*h* says even the people there are broken. But that's not true, is it? I'm still all in one piece!"

We'd run out of gas. And we had no money to refuel. We needed our last few coins to buy food.

"We'll leave the tractor here then," I said.

"But . . ."

"Get me down. And quickly."

Jadran's back was even more hunched than usual. He was trembling.

"Mika's going to be so mad," he said. "She'll never let me plow the potato patch again."

The boys with the skateboards had spotted us now too. They came our way, curiously.

"Grab the wheelchair and the gym bag," I said. "Before someone starts asking awkward questions."

Jadran's arms were shaking, but he did as I asked. He opened up the wheelchair and helped me into it. Sprig wanted to escape into the park. I only just managed to block his path and lift him back up onto my lap.

"What's wrong with him?" asked one of the boys.

I was just about to say that there was absolutely nothing wrong with Jadran, that he was very, very good at being himself. Until I realized that it wasn't me he'd asked the question to, but my brother. As if, because I was in a wheelchair, I could no longer answer for myself.

"Is he, like, paralyzed or something?"

Jadran looked a bit embarrassed and hung the gym bag on one of the handles.

"He fell," he said.

"What about that bird?"

"He didn't fall."

The boys laughed as if Jadran had meant to make a joke.

"Sprig lost his family," he said. "We're taking him home."

I thumped Jadran's back and said quickly, "He's taking me home, he means. Bye!"

I rolled around the corner. Jadran trudged after me.

"You heard that too, didn't you?" he said.

I looked over my shoulder. "Heard what?"

"They think I'm your counselor. I'm your Mika!" Jadran said with a wink. With his skinny little moustache and his big body, he looked like he was twenty. And a wolf tattoo on his wrist would look pretty good on him too.

"Keep up the good work, Giant," I said. "And I'll act all sorry for myself."

Jadran proudly pushed the wheelchair.

"I'm going to pamper you, little guy!" he said in Mika's raspy voice. "I'm super stoked with you!"

Jadran politely said hello to the passersby, and stopped now and then to check that I was sitting comfortably. He adjusted the height of the footrests and rolled the leg of my pants down over my plaster cast.

For just a little while, I really was his little brother.

You're on the news.

The screen of the telephone flashed.

A man claims he saw you. He called Jadran a "dangerous madman." Can you imagine? And he lives almost a hundred miles from here! What are you two up to?

Behind me, my brother tirelessly pushed the wheelchair, even though it was still such an impossibly long way to the place where the cranes spent the winter. He was determined to continue our journey at all costs, even without the tractor.

My fingers were freezing. I had trouble spelling the words right.

Tell mom they need to stop looking. This is something between me and Giant.

I put my hand over the screen and tried to type as discreetly as possible. Jadran didn't need to know everything that Yasmin was writing to me.

Sorry.

-Sorry?

For being annoying sometimes.

But Jadran wanted to know everything. He leaned over my shoulder so that he could read along. "Who wrote that?"

"Yasmin."

Her words were vibrating in my hand.

It's quiet here without you guys.

Jadran clicked his tongue. "She misses us."

I looked up. "Do you think so?"

"Yaz is making us better than we are, huh?" he said. "When you miss someone, you make them better than they are. Inside your head."

"You didn't come up with that yourself!"

"Mika said it. When she showed me that room."

I quickly typed an *X* and turned off the phone.

"I don't want to be inside Yasmin's head," I said.

We bought some fries and soda at a stall. Sheltered by a bus stop, we warmed ourselves on the hot bag of fries. Sprig pattered about the square, looking for something edible. The mayonnaise dripped off Jadran's fingers. I gave him my paper napkin too.

"It's about time," he murmured.

"High time," I said.

Jadran tipped half a can of soda into his mouth. I took a swig too and lifted up my chin. Then we gargled as hard as we could. Jadran sprayed soda all over his jacket.

We stayed sitting there for quite a while. It had started to drizzle, and the rain was blowing against the glass of the bus stop. Sprig pecked at the last bit of mayonnaise. A bus came trundling slowly toward us.

"Don't stand up," I whispered. "Look like you're getting the dirt out from under your fingernails."

The bus pulled up at the stop. The doors opened. A couple got out at the back. Luckily, they only had eyes for each other.

"Want me to help you in?" the driver shouted down at me, already standing up to get off the bus.

I shook my head without really looking at him.

"We're, um, staying nearby," I said.

A car was waiting on the other side of the street. It was too dark to see the driver, but it was definitely exactly the same kind of Volvo as that afternoon at the sunken road. The windshield wipers were swishing back and forth. I hardly dared to move. The car didn't drive on until just after the bus left.

"We need to find somewhere to sleep," I said quickly when the car had disappeared around the corner.

"I'm not tired yet," said Jadran.

"It's raining."

"A bit of rain's not a problem."

"Come on, Jadran. My leg hurts. I only just got out of the hospital, or did you forget again?"

"I'm your Mika, aren't I? I have to take care of you, Josh."

I peered around to see if the Volvo had stopped and was lurking somewhere, but there was no sign of it. By the light of the streetlamps, two jackdaws fought over a French fry.

That night we slept on a boat.

We'd walked for a long time, looking for a good place. My trousers were sticking to my legs because of the rain, and I thought my plaster cast might be getting soft. Sprig looked like a drowned puppy dog. Jadran had also started to moan that he wanted a real hotel this time, with a shower and a double bed.

"And soap," he said. "You have to wash your hands three times a day, Mom says."

For the first time since we'd run away, I longed to go home. To my own little hollow in the mattress.

We came to an alley with garages on both sides. One of the garage doors was slightly open. Jadran pushed it up, and we were able to slip inside.

An old sailboat was kept inside the garage. The mast had been taken off, and the garage stank of varnish and brushes. In the corner was a sink and a tub full of soft soap. And there was even an electric fan heater so that we could blow the worst of the cold out of our clothes. It was almost as good as a hotel, I thought.

Sprig snuggled down next to the heater. Jadran suggested that we should climb inside the boat. The folded sail lay on the bottom like a thin mattress.

"You can start," he said when I was finally lying comfortably.

I played the breathing game as it was meant to be played. First I breathed really slowly, and then faster and faster. And Jadran had no difficulty at all keeping up with me.

We breathed like a breeze. We breathed like a hurricane.

We breathed with shivers. We breathed deep and hard.

But most of all: we breathed together.

In and out. Chest and belly.

And breathing out, like a gust of wind over each other's faces.

Psssssbbbbbb.

IT WAS STILL PITCH DARK in the boat, but I was wide awake. I took out Yasmin's smartphone from my jacket, which was hanging to dry over the edge of the boat. I saw that she'd sent me another message in the night.

Didn't know you snorkel.

I felt a weird shiver. My diving stuff was at the bottom of my wardrobe. So Yasmin had been rummaging around in my underwear! I thought it was stupid answering at this time of day, but I did it anyway.

What were you doing in my wardrobe?

Yasmin answered almost immediately. Like she'd been waiting for my message all night.

Looking for a belt. But do you do it often?

-What? Wear a belt?

Snorkeling!

What I really wanted to do was turn off the phone. It was better to conserve the battery anyway. But I couldn't. Somehow it made me feel safe to know that at least one person was aware that we hadn't disappeared off the face of the earth.

I have a diving mask and flippers, but I hardly ever use them. Jadran gets mad when he can't come to diving club with me. And they're no use in the paddling pool with him.

I looked at my brother, who was tossing and turning in his sleep. His eyelids were twitching nervously.

What about me? Can I come with you? Snorkeling sounds like fun.

I thought about water. Glistening, open water. And the unknown world under the surface.

OK, but keep out of my stuff.

Then, for a short while, I put the telephone between me and my brother as a light, like a sort of candle.

A cold, blue candle.

Soon Jadran was awake too. He sat up straight and ran his hands through his messy hair, like there was something stuck inside his head that he wanted to scratch loose.

"Bad dream?" I asked.

"I can't stop thinking about it," he said.

"You mean the Space?"

"The wings. I smashed them, didn't I? They're completely broken."

"Doesn't matter, Giant. Mom had almost forgotten about them."

That wasn't what Jadran wanted to hear. He stamped his feet on the wooden floor of the boat.

"Now Dad will never come back!" he wailed.

"He won't come back anyway," I said. "I'm sorry. But even Mom's hardly seen him since."

Jadran pushed down the blanket. The astronaut on his new pajamas was made of luminous material. It glowed in the dark.

He said, "Dad was in love with Mom because she danced so beautifully with those blue wings on. And now I've broken them! It's all my fault, isn't it?"

I sighed. The light of the telephone had gone out.

"What stinks so bad?" I asked, changing the subject.

Luckily, Jadran could smell it too. He climbed out of the boat and switched on the fluorescent light.

It was Sprig. He was completely covered in diarrhea. The down on his belly and butt was stuck together.

"That's what you get for eating all that mayonnaise," I said.

Jadran grabbed a towel and walked toward Sprig.

"Don't do that, Giant. He's filthy!"

"I have two patients now." He sounded almost proud. "I'll look after both of you. I'm a great nurse, huh?"

Jadran stood at the sink and rinsed Sprig's legs. He ran his fingers through the down and washed out the mess. Before long, his new pajamas were covered in bird poop too, but it was still wonderful to see my brother busily working away.

"And now you!" Jadran put a load of soft soap on his hand and climbed into the boat. "Pull down your pants."

"Stop it!" I shrieked.

"Do as you're told, Josh."

"No way!"

"Off with your underpants. Then I can wash your butt too."

Then Jadran aimed the blob of soap at my head. I ducked out of the way just in time. He screamed with laughter.

HALF AN HOUR LATER, WE were back on the road. Jadran pushed the wheelchair and set quite a pace. With every step, he blew a cloud of breath onto the back of my neck. I lay the blanket over Sprig's damp feathers. He wasn't squeaking like usual and the whistle in his throat seemed broken too.

From the alley with the garages, we followed a wide avenue that led to the outskirts of the town. It was still early. There were hardly any other people around.

We passed a big, empty building with a tall fence around it. There'd be hundreds of kids swarming together here again soon. They'd be playing soccer and telling one another all the stuff they'd done during the fall break.

"It's Monday," I said.

"On Monday we go swimming," said Jadran.

"But not today."

"First we'll take Sprig home. And then we'll go swimming together, right?"

Jadran beamed as if he wanted to assure me that we could walk to Spain and back, just in one day.

I thought about what I'd promised Yasmin. It was going to be months before I could do a good kick with my broken leg again.

In the dawn light, a cloud of thrushes passed over us. Sprig was still too frozen to look up at the hundreds of birds. But Jadran saw them.

"We have to go that way!" he shouted.

"Maybe you still can catch up with them," I said to fire him up a bit.

Jadran hadn't been expecting that. For a moment, he hesitated, and then he pushed the wheelchair with full force after the birds. The wheels grated on the concrete as we went around the corner. There were bags of garbage all over the sidewalk, but Jadran skillfully zigzagged between them. Even after the thrushes had disappeared over the roofs, he went on running.

"I'm the horse and you're the carriage!" He whinnied.

"Then we should be the other way around. The horse goes in front of the carriage."

Jadran turned the wheelchair and stood between the two handles so that he could pull me along. He galloped off down the street. I looked back the way we'd come.

Jadran kept going until we'd left the town behind.

That was when I saw the Volvo again. The red car was slowly following us. Sometimes it stopped at the roadside and waited until I could hardly see it. Then it drove forward a bit, turned down a side street, and reappeared out of the next one.

Now I was sure of it: We were being followed.

Maybe it's Murad, I suddenly thought. But then why was he waiting so long to step in?

A shivery sensation ran down my spine. Or maybe it was Dad!

It had to be Dad! Even though he lived in Russia now. It must have been such a shock for him when he saw our photos and heard that we'd run away from home. So he'd jumped on the first plane. But how had he found us so quickly?

Jadran wasn't paying attention to the Volvo. Which was just as well. I had no idea how he'd react if he knew someone was on our trail. But I was sure he'd blow his fuse.

I looked back again. There was no sign of the Volvo.

"You can slow down a bit now." I did my best to sound as normal as possible.

"Slow is for snails," replied Jadran, throwing his

full weight behind the wheelchair. Startled, Sprig spread his wet wings and took off.

"Hey, Giant!" I was almost catapulted onto the ground.

Just when I'd settled back into the wheelchair, the phone beeped. I fished it out of my jacket. The battery was at thirty percent. Would Yasmin never stop sending me these messages?

> It works perfectly! I just went in the bathtub with your mask and that tube. I could see my toes underwater. X.

I reread the words three times. And every time I felt colder.

Suddenly I understood everything. I couldn't believe I hadn't realized before! I'd answered Yasmin very early this morning, and now that Volvo had turned up again. It couldn't be a coincidence. Every time I sent her a message, the police could track the signal. I'd seen them do it on TV. And so the driver of the Volvo knew exactly where we were.

I'd almost fallen for it. Yasmin wasn't really worried about us. She didn't want to go snorkeling with me at all. Her *X* wasn't a kiss. It was a bomb, like in a game of Battleship. As long as Yasmin kept planting crosses, they could find us in no time.

And I'd had enough of it.

I'm onto you! This is my last message, you traitor!

There was a creek at the side of the road. The water was covered with dry leaves.

"Look, Giant!" I shouted. "Sprig is looping the loop."

Jadran turned his head to look at Sprig, who was floating on the wind.

I aimed Yasmin's telephone and tossed it into the creek. It landed on the leaves and lay there until the blue light went out.

Then it sank, trailing bubbles in its wake.

"WHAT TIME IS IT?" ASKED Jadran.

"Twenty-three minutes to eight," I guessed.

"Then I'm hungry!" Jadran raced on like a rabid bear. "I've been hungry for seven minutes!"

We saw a store along the road. Jadran sprinted all the way and rushed into the parking lot. The little supermarket was about to open. Sprig landed on the roof and ruffled his feathers. He still hadn't entirely recovered from being sick.

Jadran parked the wheelchair in front of the glass doors and paced up and down. He rattled off the list of his regular breakfast items: "Bread, white and brown. Jam. Chocolate milk."

"Money," I said.

"You can't eat money."

"We've almost run out."

Jadran counted the coins he still had left. Behind

us, a car turned into the parking lot. I didn't even have to look to know which car it was. I caught a glimpse of the driver in the side mirror. That black hat. The fur collar. But for the first time I also clearly saw a face.

It was a narrow face with big, expressive eyes. The driver of the Volvo was not Dad or Murad.

It was a woman.

And she knew us only too well.

The lights inside the store went on. Jadran pressed his nose to the glass. I was shaking, but I knew I really had to think of something.

"I don't want to go in there in the wheelchair," I said. "I want to walk."

Jadran frowned as if I'd just said something really dumb.

"On one leg?"

"Go on, Giant. If you help me, it'll work. I have to practice, Dr. Mbasa said. And you're my number one nurse."

Jadran snapped out of it. He hooked his arm into mine and pulled me up. It was really painful and for a moment I thought my injured ankle was going to crumple. But he held me up.

"Good job, little guy," he said. "You can do it!"

Hanging onto Jadran, I limped into the store. The wheelchair stayed outside next to a bicycle rack, so that our pursuer could clearly see that we were inside. Jadran pawed at just about all of the bread rolls and pastries, before finally choosing a packet of chocolate bars.

When we'd paid, I said we'd better take the exit at the back of the building. That way at least we'd stay out of sight of the Volvo. Jadran didn't usually get too many chocolate bars, and he was so happy that he didn't ask any questions.

There was a discarded shopping cart by the door, which came in handy.

"Help me get into that cart," I said. "It'll be faster."

Jadran already had his fingers in the packet of chocolate bars. Stuffing one of them into his mouth, he lifted me into the cart. It was really uncomfortable. My leg stuck up and out at an angle, like a flagpole.

"And now let's get outta here!"

Jadran had no idea what was going on. "What about the wheelchair?"

"We'll come get it later."

Luckily he didn't object. We followed a street at the back of the supermarket. The wheels of the cart jerked about on the rough surface.

I didn't dare to look back until the supermarket was some way behind us. In the parking lot, I could just make out the back of the Volvo.

"You're acting weird," said Jadran. "Something's up, isn't it? Something I'm not allowed to know about."

"You're always allowed to know everything, Giant."

"So why did you want to get into this shopping cart?"

"Oh, you know, I just . . ."

"You think I'm dumb."

I clasped my fingers around the metal wire. "Okay, then, if you really want to know, I think someone's watching us."

Jadran clapped his hands. "You see! I saw right through you, Josh. Everyone knows you're in a wheelchair. It's too obvious. That's why you left it behind!"

I sighed and smiled at the same time. "Right again, Giant. The wheelchair was way too noticeable. And that's why I'm jammed into a shopping cart now."

The street went more to the west than the south. But I didn't know if that really mattered. Our goal seemed farther away than ever. And I wasn't going to be able to put up with being folded in two inside a shopping cart for long.

"Where's Sprig?" asked Jadran after he'd gobbled down his fifth chocolate bar.

I couldn't believe I'd forgotten about him! All that

business with the Volvo and the shopping cart had made me completely lose sight of the crane.

"He'll be flying after us somewhere," I said.

Jadran swung the cart around with a jolt. The branches of the oak trees along the side of the road were swaying back and forth. There was no sign of a bird in the sky above us.

"We forgot him," said Jadran.

"He'll find us."

Jadran shook his head. "Sprig doesn't know where the south is. You saw that for yourself, didn't you? He'll get lost!"

Jadran pushed the shopping cart back in the direction we'd come from.

"Wait. We can't go back. We're being followed, Giant. Someone's coming after us."

"How do you know that?" he asked.

"I saw them. Yesterday at that sunken road. Last night at the bus stop. And back there in the parking lot. It's always the same red car. Someone's watching us."

Jadran tightened his lips. "You saw them. And you didn't say anything?"

"I wanted to tell you, Giant. But . . ."

Jadran pushed down on the handle with his full weight and lifted the shopping cart up on its back wheels. I tilted back, with my legs in the air.

"Brothers always tell each other everything!" he

shouted. I was scared stiff. His voice sounded as deep and powerful as when he copied Dad. "We do everything together!"

The shopping cart crashed onto its four wheels. My plaster cast bounced onto the metal edge. Jadran hunched over the handle and started muttering to himself. I knew that I'd better not ask him anything.

I breathed in deep and blew warm air over my hands. I tried to kid myself that I wasn't absolutely freezing.

And then suddenly there they were. The trumpets sounded out of nowhere.

Krrroo krrroo krrroo!

At first there were just a few cranes, but before long they were hanging in a big group above us. Jadran and I looked up at almost the same time. The shadows of the birds left dark trails on the grass.

"Is that Sprig?" I asked. "Has he flown away with them?"

Krrroo krrroo krrroo-ee!

It was impossible to recognize Sprig among all those birds. And we couldn't hear his squeaking either because of all the noise.

We gazed at the flapping wings. Jadran gulped when one of the birds dropped to the back of the group and another one caught the wind and flew up front. He read the letters they were writing.

The big crane ABC.

He plucked their words out of the sky.

"Sprig!" he screamed. "Wait for us, Sprig! We're coming too!"

JADRAN SLIPPED TO THE GROUND and sat leaning against the shopping cart. He banged the back of his head against the bars.

Boom! Boom!

"Stop that, Giant!" I shouted. "We don't even know if Sprig was with those cranes."

"Bye," mumbled Jadran. "He didn't even say goodbye." He stood back up, took hold of the handle of the cart, and, with a jerk, swung it around on its axis.

"Let go of the cart!" I braced myself and tried to scramble out, but I fell back into the cart. Breathing calmly wasn't going to help soothe Jadran now. And Mom's soft little words certainly wouldn't do any good.

"I'm not going back!" He pounded on the handle of the cart. "I don't want to be in the room next to Guillaume's."

"Of course we're not going back! Just help me get

out of the cart. Then we can think about what we're going to do."

But Jadran tipped the shopping cart onto its back wheels again and spun it wildly around. I went slamming into the side.

"You're hurting me!" I turned around and bashed his hands with my fists so that he'd have to let go of the shopping cart. But he just grasped the handle even more tightly.

Jadran turned the cart in a circle on the asphalt. I jolted back and forth. The plaster creaked. He was spinning me around so fast that I felt sick. I was in a vortex.

Jadran's own little tornado.

"Lemme out!" I screamed.

I thought I was going to puke.

Jadran suddenly stopped turning around and let the cart thud to a stop. His face brightened up. He blinked a few times and then swallowed.

"I'm going to miss you, Max," he said in Mom's clear voice.

"I'll miss you too," he made Dad reply. "But I want to move on."

"And what's going to happen to Jadran?" whispered Mom. "And little Josh? He'll be able to talk soon!"

Jadran came and stood next to me, leaned over the edge of the cart, and looked at me like I was an infant in a stroller. He looked like Dad, I noticed for the first time, with that frown and the hint of a moustache.

Jadran reached out his hand and gently stroked my neck. But it was not his hand that was touching me.

Those soft fingers belonged to Dad.

We were startled by a loud honking. Jadran looked up, annoyed. I quickly pushed away his hand.

"Move!" I said. "The cart's blocking the way!"

But this car did not want to go past. The red Volvo parked and flashed its lights. The door swung open. A woman in an army jacket got out.

"M-M-Mika?" stammered Jadran.

She walked toward us with her arms open wide. The wolf on her wrist was howling.

"Hey, guys!" she said. "I'm stoked to see you two." She gave me a wink, but she looked really, really worried.

The magnet did its job. Jadran finally let go of the cart and threw his arms around Mika.

"Me too," he said. "I'm stoked too. And you too, huh? We're always stoked to see Mika."

Mika stroked her hand over my plastered leg, which was sticking out of the shopping cart.

"You okay?" she asked.

"You were . . . just in time," I groaned. I felt like crying, but I was too shaken up for that.

"Come on, I'll rescue you from this cage," she said.

Mika opened up the trunk and took out the wheelchair. Then she slid her arm under my armpit, just like she'd done when we found Jadran at the lake.

"Give me a hand?" she asked my brother.

He didn't have to be asked twice. Together they lifted me out of the shopping cart. He didn't even seem surprised to see Mika turn up here. Just a minute ago he'd been a wild man and now he was acting like an excited little kid again.

He started rattling away. "Sprig's gone. He went with the cranes. He's left us behind, hasn't he? And we've already come so far!"

"I don't think so," said Mika. "He likes you way too much for that."

Jadran laughed sheepishly. "Do you know where he is then?"

"He's waiting for you guys." Mika nodded toward the supermarket. "Over there on the roof. Like a good little puppy dog."

Jadran looked at me, beaming. "Sprig's not gone. He likes me way too much, huh?"

I didn't know what to do with my face.

Mika pushed the wheelchair toward the supermarket. Jadran ran ahead of us with the shopping cart. It was almost impossible to keep up with him.

"It was you," I said to Mika when I was sure my brother wouldn't hear us. "You saw us at that sunken road."

Mika just nodded. She tightened her scarf around her neck.

"You found us ages ago, so why didn't you do something? Everyone was looking for us. Even the police . . ."

Mika stopped and crouched next to the wheelchair.

"I was supposed to stop you," she whispered. "But I couldn't do it. The two of you looked so . . . together. So wonderfully together. I was scared I might break something. It was doing Jadran good, and I hadn't seen him so self-confident for a long time."

My brother skipped ahead of us. He put his feet on the base of the shopping cart and rolled away down the street.

"You could have let Mom know," I said.

"What do you think I've been doing? She calls me three times a day."

"So she knows?" I could hardly believe her.

"Not everything. I told her I was following you and that there was no need for her to worry. Everything still seemed to be going okay, and I definitely didn't want to force you to do anything. I told her to ask the police to stay out of it for the time being. That would get Jadran too excited. And she knew I'd step in at the right moment."

"And that moment's now?" I slumped in the wheelchair.

Mika stood up and started pushing me again. "I actually wanted to stop you last night at the bus stop. But then I got a call and I lost the two of you. I didn't have the tractor to follow anymore, and I couldn't see the crane in the dark. I didn't dare tell your mom. I just drove around crying all night."

"But then how did you find us again?" I asked, although the answer wasn't hard to guess.

"Yasmin," we both said almost at the same moment.

"This morning I called your place. I wanted to explain to your mom what had happened, but Yasmin answered. She heard that I was panicking and she tried to comfort me. And then she let on that she'd been in touch with you the entire time."

"Ha! I knew it!" I slid forward to the edge of the

seat. "Yasmin wasn't just sending me those messages for no reason. The police picked up the signal every time I replied. So of course you could find us."

Mika chuckled. "Yasmin didn't need the police for that. She can trace her smartphone easily with the computer if it's lost—or if someone else has run off with it."

I could hardly breathe. So Yasmin knew exactly where we were? And she'd been following us the whole time? In the trees beside the road, some crows were cawing pushily. I wished I could swat them away.

"What now?" I asked Mika. "Will you let us finish our journey? We'll go get Sprig and then . . ."

Mika put her hand on my shoulder. Her fingers were warm but firm.

She said, "What Jadran just did back there, swinging you around in that shopping cart, I really can't let anything like that happen. He needs help. Professional help."

I leaned my head toward her arm. The tattoo of the wolf touched my ear. I could hear it growling and howling at the same time.

"You're doing fantastically well with your big brother, Josh. But let me help you now—please."

At the far end of the parking lot, Jadran was taking a running start. He jumped onto the cart again and rattled off down the road.

I tried to look back at Mika behind the wheelchair, but the sun blasted me in the face.

All I could see was patches of blue.

Two big, flapping patches of blue.

SPRIG FLAPPED HIS WINGS. HE was perched like a weathercock on the top of the radio tower next to the supermarket. As soon as he saw my brother, he stretched his neck, but he still did not make a sound.

Jadran stopped the shopping cart from rolling and ran into the parking lot, right up to the foot of the radio tower.

"Sprig! Sprig!" He straightened his back, flapped his arms, and stuck out his butt. "Come down, Sprig! We need to get going! We're taking you to your family!"

Mika cursed under her breath when she heard Jadran shouting. She crouched next to the wheelchair. "Will you tell him, Josh?"

"Huh? What do you mean?" I said, even though I understood perfectly well.

"I can lure your brother into the car with some kind of trick and drive off with him, but that's not how

I want to do it. It's important that he understands why we're doing this. You have the best chance of persuading him, Josh. He stopped listening to your mother ages ago, and I . . ."

"But . . ." My face must have looked pathetic.

"Do it, Josh. Please. Think of your mom, and Murad and Yasmin."

"I don't care about Yasmin!"

Mika's wolf bared its teeth. "Or about what really is best for all of you."

We both looked at Jadran, who was yelling at Sprig now. He was stamping, flapping his wings, bowing his head as deep as he could. He was dancing like a happy crane, high on his toes and sticking his head forward.

"I don't know if I can . . ."

"Tell him we're leaving in five minutes. I'll go fetch the car. And don't you dare run off again. I trust you, Josh."

Mika turned to go to the place where she'd left the Volvo. She stopped and looked back one last time.

"Sorry," she said. "It was a crazy trip. But it stops here." Then she took her phone and tapped in a number.

I rolled the wheelchair to the foot of the radio tower, to where my brother was. This was our last chance to escape. Mika was going to fetch the car. If we were quick enough, then . . .

"Mika's taking us with her, isn't she?" said Jadran even before I could say anything. "She wants us to go back. That's why she's here."

I shook my head and nodded at the same time. "We have to go home, Giant. Enough is enough. Come on."

Jadran kicked the metal of the tower. "I'm not allowed to go home! I have to go live in a different room. The room next to Guillaume's."

If we wanted to escape, then we had to do it now. But I couldn't.

"We tried, Giant, but it didn't work. We're out of food, and the tractor's broken. We have to go back."

I spoke Mika's words as though I'd come up with them myself.

Jadran put one foot on the narrow ladder that ran up the side of the tower. His whole body was shaking.

"I'm staying with you," he said.

"And I'm staying with you, Giant, even if you're sleeping somewhere else. And Mika will take such good care of you. She promised."

The red Volvo drove into the parking lot.

"Mika's splitting us up!" Jadran shook his head and climbed onto the first rung.

"No, Giant, she's not. She says it's better for everyone if . . ."

Jadran sniffed. With every gulp of air, he climbed

a rung higher. Sprig twitched his beak nervously as if he was trying to lure him to the top.

I slid to the edge of the wheelchair and pushed myself to my feet. Grabbing the ladder, I put the foot of my good leg on the bottom rung. A knife jabbed into my ankle, but I pulled myself up. I couldn't bend the plaster cast, so my arms had to do all the work. I kept it up for three rungs. Then it felt like my muscles were about to snap.

"It's too dangerous, Giant!" I shouted, as I sank back into the wheelchair.

Jadran paid no attention to me and just kept climbing higher and higher. Sprig let go and flew in big circles around the tower.

"Jadran, come down here right now!" screamed Mika.

I'd never seen her like that before. The wolf was in her throat now too. It growled threateningly. She grabbed onto the ladder. If the mast was a tree, she'd have shaken Jadran right out of it.

Jadran looked down and grinned a challenge. He dared to do anything. Up that narrow ladder, all the way to the top. Not once did his feet miss a rung. Not once did he loosen his grip. Sprig wheeled around him.

"I'm staying here!" he whooped. "I don't want a room with a bathroom. Come get me if you can!"

For the first time in all those days I realized Mika was right. I didn't know how to help him anymore. I couldn't keep him safe. But maybe the people at the Space could.

"I messed up," I said to Mika. "Mom says I'm Jadran's guardian angel. But I get everything wrong."

Mika looked at Jadran, who was yelling away at the top of the radio tower, and then she looked at me. The wolf was hiding under her sleeve again.

"If anything is messed up, we all did it together," she said. "Whether we like it or not, we're one another's guardian angels. All of us."

Always

IT WASN'T A WEATHERCOCK UP there at the top of the tower. And it wasn't a crane. It was my brother. My sweet, unrelentingly irritating brother. He'd been up there for almost three long hours.

And this time it was all my fault. Mika could try to calm me down as much as she liked, but I was the one who'd driven him up there by stupidly asking him to stop. I'd said to him that it was actually better if he moved. For him. For us. That meant I'd abandoned my brother, I knew that. I screamed myself hoarse and made the highest breathing bridge in the world, but Jadran didn't budge.

A big group of people stood by the supermarket, watching to see what would happen. There were police cars, an ambulance, and, at the back of the parking lot, the blue lights of the ladder truck were flashing. Sprig flew silently above the radio tower. The commotion was probably scaring him.

Mom, Murad, and Yasmin had just arrived. We were more than 180 miles from home, Murad told me. It wasn't as far as Jadran and I had hoped, but it was still a long way toward the south. Mom had sped like crazy to get here.

Now she was standing next to me, clasping the arm of the wheelchair with one hand. I could feel her shaking through the metal. If Jadran fell from the tower, then we'd need more than a miracle.

"Come on, Giant! Let's make friends again!"

Her voice sounded tired and hoarse.

Jadran pretended not to hear her.

Yasmin was holding Murad's hand. I couldn't see her eyes clearly because of the reflection on her glasses, but I could feel that she was looking at me. I turned my head away. What did she want? Yasmin had betrayed us at the last moment. Sending messages with *X*'s in them. Claiming she missed us. And that she wanted to go snorkeling with me! And meanwhile she was blabbing to Mika about where exactly we were . . .

Murad let go of Yasmin's hand. He put one hand on my shoulder and the other on Mom's.

"We have to fetch something from the car," he said. He squeezed both of our shoulders at the same time, as if he deliberately wanted to leave us alone for a bit. Then he and Yasmin disappeared among the cars in the parking lot.

Mom forced a smile. Her flowery perfume made my nose sting.

"You still mad at me, Little Giant?" I could tell she'd practiced that line with Murad in the car.

I pulled myself away. I did not want to have this conversation. Of course I'd been really mad at Mom, because of what she wanted to do to Jadran. But at the same time I was also happy that she was here with me now. Stoked, even. But that wasn't going to be easy for me to explain.

Mom had once said to me that talking is like shedding a skin. But there wasn't a new skin ready beneath my old one.

The ladder truck drove up to the radio tower. Mika climbed into the bucket with a firefighter. The ladder extended with a buzzing sound. Everyone fell silent.

The ladder reached up high, but not quite high enough to get to Jadran. Mika and the firefighter waved their arms. They tried to persuade him and signaled at him to come down a bit lower, down to the safety of the bucket.

Jadran stared in the opposite direction.

Mom was hesitating. She smoothed the creases out of her coat.

"Do you think you can persuade him?" she asked.

I shook my head and looked at the fire truck. The ladder slid back down. Mika stepped out and walked over to Mom.

"Sorry, Margot," she said. "I don't know what else to do. He's being more stubborn than ever."

Murad came walking back toward us too. Yasmin trudged after him with a lumpy black package in her arms. I recognized the garment bag instantly.

Without saying anything, Yasmin unzipped the bag.

There was that beautiful blue again.

The hundreds of feathers.

Very carefully, she took out the wings.

They looked just as impressive as they had before. They were just as soft and just as fluffy on the underside. All the flight feathers were back in place. There was no sign of the bare wire anywhere and the buckles had been polished. On one side, the worn-out shoulder strap had been replaced by a new bright-green leather belt. It was the belt from my wardrobe. And it fit perfectly.

Murad folded the empty bag in two over his arm.

"Yaz worked on it with the patience of a saint,"

he said. "While we were looking all over for you and Jadran, she's been sewing day and night."

Yasmin didn't wait for Mom or Mika to tell her what to do. She walked over to the ladder truck with the wings and climbed confidently into the bucket. The firefighter looked questioningly in our direction. Murad nodded that it was okay. There was a rattling of cables and motors. The bucket went up—with Yasmin in it.

I'd have so loved to see the look on Jadran's face when he realized the wings had been repaired. But he was too far away.

Yasmin lifted the wings above her head. The wind ruffled the feathers. In the bright daylight they looked even bluer than usual.

And that was when Jadran finally started moving. He carefully went down a rung. Mom squeezed my arm.

Slowly, he lowered himself to the bucket. And all the while Yasmin held out the wings in front of her. Sprig did a nose dive, as if he wanted to warn Jadran. But Jadran only had eyes for one thing.

Gently, he put one foot on the edge of the bucket. He let go with one hand and grabbed the rail next to Yasmin. For a second, he hung halfway between the tower and the ladder truck.

Mom held her breath. And I stopped breathing too.

We blew out again, at exactly the same moment.

Pffffff.

Jadran jumped in next to Yasmin and pulled the wings out of her hands.

He was an angel.

A giant blue angel, high in the sky.

Yasmin buckled the tips of the wings around his wrists. Jadran spread his wings triumphantly, almost knocking her over. Sprig circled above them.

Next to me, Mom stared speechlessly at the magnificent creature that was slowly descending.

MIKA HAD ARRANGED FOR US to stay at a nearby hotel. We were going there for a hot bath and a night's rest. Meanwhile, Murad would take Jadran's stuff to his new room at the Space. Then he could go straight there tomorrow morning.

Mom was trying to calm Jadran down on a sofa in the hotel lobby. He jumped back to his feet and paced up and down past the reception desk. The blue wings were still attached to his back, but he was walking with more of a hunch than ever before.

"Sprig needs us," he raged. "He doesn't know anything about the south! We saw that for ourselves, didn't we, Josh? He flew completely the wrong way."

"That crane will be fine," said Mika. "He'll leave with the next group that flies over, don't you worry. He's still a wild animal, after all."

"I want to sleep on the roof!" roared Jadran.

The girl behind the reception desk acted like nothing was going on.

"Okay," said Mika. "Jadran will sleep on the roof, and you two can take the nearest room."

She winked at me and Mom. The medication would start to work soon. Mika had already given it to Jadran in a cup of chocolate milk. Any minute now he'd have that thick tongue and zombie eyes again. Usually I hated seeing my brother like that. But this time, it would be good. I just wanted some food and a real bed.

After Jadran had calmed down and Mika had reassured them that everything was under control, Murad and Yasmin got ready to leave for home.

Yasmin came toward me. I didn't know whether to thank her or yell at her. Admittedly, she had gotten Jadran down from the radio tower, but then she was the one who . . .

"You stopped answering me," she said.

"What did you expect? Do you think I didn't know what you were up to with your fake messages?"

"Fake? What do you mean? I meant everything I wrote."

"You betrayed us to Mika!"

"I didn't betray anything," she snapped. "I was just trying to help. Mika was really upset, so I had to tell her something! We were scared, Josh. Scared something bad might happen to the two of you."

I understood that, but I didn't reply. I thought about how far we would have gotten if Yasmin hadn't given the game away at the last moment. Jadran would have pushed the wheelchair all the way to Spain.

Or maybe not.

"By the way, where's my phone now?" asked Yasmin.

I kept my cool, but all my muscles went limp. "You can just trace it yourself, can't you? You were watching us the whole time!"

"The signal's dead." Yasmin's eyes flashed fire under her black bangs.

"Lost it," I said quickly, before she could burn me.

"Lost it?"

"In the creek."

She rolled her lips over each other. The fire went out.

"Sorry," I mumbled.

"You wanted to get rid of me. You don't want me snorkeling with you at all."

Murad waved her over. She shrugged and went after him. Her sneakers squeaked on the tiled floor.

"Yaz?" I called when she already had one foot out the door. "I . . ."

She instantly turned to look at me, as if she had been waiting for me to speak. "Yes?" She took a step back. The sliding doors closed behind her.

"Err . . . Thanks for the wings."

Yasmin took off her glasses and breathed on the lenses.

"Why did you actually repair them?" I asked. "I thought you hated us."

She rubbed the lenses on her sleeve, put the glasses back on, and looked to make sure that Murad couldn't hear us.

She said, "I was sick of the whole moving-in thing. My dad tries so hard, for you and Jadran, for Margot. He wants to make everyone happy. But do you think I chose this?"

I looked at Yasmin. For the first time I noticed how soft and dark her eyelashes were, under those straight bangs.

"Maybe I'd have liked to run away too," she said. "To close the door behind me and then run away as far as possible, out of town, to someplace I didn't know."

The sliding doors opened again. Murad was coming to see where she was. Yasmin gave me a quick wave and followed him outside.

"I'd rather you stayed with us," I whispered as she left.

We had lasagna in the hotel bar. Jadran was too groggy to gobble it down. Mika didn't sit at the same table as us, but instead went and read a magazine by the door. Even now she was still shadowing us.

Mom still didn't entirely understand why we wanted to escape on that tractor of all things.

"It was a crazy plan, Josh. You should have stopped your brother." Her voice was small and shaky, but her eyes were fuming.

"Giant is sixteen!"

"And tomorrow we're going back to the hospital. Dr. Mbasa says you have to rest. To lie still. Three fractures, Josh! And then the two of you just go and run away on a tractor . . ."

Jadran dropped his cutlery on the table with a clatter.

"The airplane," he said.

"Just eat your dinner, Giant," said Mom. "There'll be no more flying today."

"I want to see it!"

"Shh, not so loud."

"He was wearing a white helmet. And he had a beak on his arm."

"Who do you mean?"

I mumbled with my mouth full, "The pilot."

"Which pilot?"

"In that video we watched for hours at the visitor

center, remember? This researcher guy flew a hang glider and the young cranes followed him. They didn't have any parents to teach them the way."

Jadran banged his hands on the table. "I want to see it!"

"Okay, fine. But keep your voice down." Mom took her smartphone out of her bag. I helped her to type in the nature center's website.

There was the hang glider again. The pilot gave a thumbs-up before taking off. It wasn't long before the first cranes were flying after him.

"Is that it?" asked Mom. "Is that why you stole that tractor, Giant? To show Sprig the way, like that man with the hang glider?"

"I didn't steal it!"

"It nearly worked," I said. "Sprig followed us the whole time."

Jadran's fork clattered onto his plate. "He needs his family, doesn't he? His daddy crane!"

In the video the young birds had flown after the hang glider in a tight *V*. They hadn't seemed to have learned any other letters yet.

Mom shook her head. "And how much farther did you think you were going to drive?"

"To his family!" shouted Jadran. He pushed back his chair and waddled drowsily to the exit of the bar. "We're taking Sprig to his family!"

But before he stepped outside, Mika grabbed his wrist.

She'd chosen the seat by the door for a reason.

WE GOT A ROOM WITH three beds. Mom slid two of them together so Jadran could lie close to me. Now that the medication was working, there wasn't going to be any sleeping on the roof.

Mom helped me out of the wheelchair. I sank deep into the mattress. My brother lay stretched out on the bed and pulled the covers over his face. He fell straight to sleep.

In the middle of the night, I woke with a start. I wasn't dreaming, but I could hear strange voices in the room.

I knew one of the voices. It was Dad, or at least Dad as imitated by Jadran. But the other one was new. It was a high-pitched woman's voice, and she was singing. Her voice was so pure and so touching that it made me feel like I was glowing. She was singing about falling in love again.

Dad answered her straightaway, singing a line back to her.

And then they both joined their voices and sang together.

I pushed myself up and saw two adult silhouettes at the window. Mom and Jadran were singing to each other. They were dancing and acting. I was in the middle of a musical.

It was crazy to see Jadran like that. He was singing like a drunkard in love, but his acting was fantastic. And he still knew half of the script of *The Blue Angel* by heart. Mom only had to quote a sentence and he'd answer immediately.

"Will you come with me then?" asked Mom.

"I'll follow you anywhere," said Jadran solemnly.

And then they waltzed between the beds and through the hotel room. Jadran leaned over Mom and stiffly led her around. They stumbled and almost fell against the wardrobe. But they were dancing. And Mom was completely wrapped up in it.

They stopped at the chair where the blue wings were hanging. Jadran picked them up and lifted them behind Mom's back.

"Go on," he said. "They're your wings."

Mom hesitated, but then put her arms through the straps. Jadran tried to fasten the buckles around Mom's wrists.

"You have to dance for me!" he said.

For a moment, Mom stood there like that, with her back to the window. She hadn't danced for years, but now she stretched her neck, opened up her arms, and darted across the room on tiptoe. Jadran leaped around after her as if she was a giant butterfly that he was trying to catch.

Suddenly he dropped down onto the bed.

"Are you okay, Giant?" Mom immediately switched the light on. The blue wings hung limply on her back again.

Jadran was breathing heavily.

"It's all my fault, isn't it?" he mumbled. "It's always my fault."

"What's your fault?" Mom slid a wing behind his back.

Jadran began to cry. It was one long succession of sobs.

"Dad was angry. He wanted to go to Russia," he said. "That was your dream, wasn't it? To perform everywhere. All over the world. But then . . ."

". . . you came along?" asked Mom.

"Yes," sobbed Jadran. "Then I came along."

Mom held her forehead to his.

She whispered, "And you are the most beautiful gift I have ever received."

Mom and Jadran came and lay next to me on the bed. I was allowed to be the baby in the middle.

"It is not your fault that it went wrong with Dad, Giant," said Mom. "And it's not Josh's either. Things hadn't been right between us for a while, you guys have to believe me. I don't know how I'd have managed without the two of you."

And then we started breathing together, all three of us at the same time, just like the old days.

Mom took the lead, Jadran followed her, and I drifted along on the rhythm of their blowing and puffing.

Every breath was a step closer together.

A step on the bridge of air that connected us forever.

AT EXACTLY HALF PAST SEVEN we got breakfast. Mom came into the room with bread rolls and fresh fruit. She slid the tray onto the bed and snuggled down between me and Jadran.

We ate lying down between the sheets. Jadran was still sluggish, and his eyes were red. But the food did him good. He'd soon be back to his old self.

When we'd finished everything, Mom put the tray on a chair. She pulled the sheets tight and brushed the crumbs onto her hand.

"Well, what are you waiting for?" she asked.

"Are we leaving already?" I said.

Mom winked. "It's a long way."

"I'm not going to the Space!" Jadran pushed off the covers.

"Is that what I said?"

"Yes!" shouted Jadran. "Yes, that's what she said, isn't it, Josh!"

Mom started stuffing all our things back into the gym bag.

"That was yesterday," she said. "But now it's today. And today we're doing everything different."

"Different and better, I hope," I said.

Mom nodded and zipped up the bag.

"But if that doesn't work, just different is a good start."

Mom had done a lot of thinking that night, she told us. She'd seen Jadran as she'd never seen him before. He'd done things she never even knew he could do, like take such good care of Sprig and me, and dance with her. And she was shocked by how badly he'd been affected by Dad leaving, because he hardly ever said anything about it.

And now Mom had a plan.

"There's still one thing we need to do," she said. "You're not finished yet, are you?"

After she'd rocked us to sleep with her breathing last night, she'd looked on her phone for the nearest place where cranes spend the winter. She'd studied maps and calculated distances.

"It's not all the way to Spain," she said. "But it's still a good place for cranes. One long day's drive and we'll be there."

Mika had stayed at the hotel too, and she told us that Jadran's new room was all ready for him. The other residents had decorated the hallway. They'd welcome him with open arms later. She didn't approve of Mom's plan at all.

"I feel responsible for him," she said. "Jadran's just had a big explosion. Now he needs some structure and some time to rest."

But Mom didn't give in.

"I know you want the best for him," she said. "But so do I. We're going to finish this journey together."

Mika sighed out the tension of the past few days.

"Then I'm coming with you," she said.

Mom shook her head. "This is something I have to do with just my two boys."

First we went and picked up Sprig in the Volvo. He was still hanging around the last place he'd seen us.

"You guys taught him to eat that junk," said Mom with a laugh when we saw him scratching around the dumpsters outside the supermarket.

Jadran lured Sprig away with some bread crumbs and held him on his lap in the car. I opened the window and put my head out. I recognized the road we'd come all the way along with the wheelchair. The place where I'd last seen the red Volvo and had even dared to believe for a moment that Dad had come to find us.

We drove past the muddy creek, where Yasmin's phone was now lying at the bottom. I felt bad for her. When I was back home, I'd start saving up for a new one.

Mika stopped at a gas station. Mom got out and came back a bit later with a heavy jerry can that she put in the trunk with our stuff.

Jadran didn't say anything the entire time. He clutched Sprig to his chest like a giant baby. And he was singing to him, I think. I saw his lips moving, even though I didn't hear anything.

We did everything in silence. Mika poured the diesel from the jerry can into the tank of the tractor. Mom took the gym bag and her own little suitcase out of the Volvo and put them next to the folded-up wheelchair in the bucket. Then they helped me into the passenger seat.

Jadran freed Sprig from the blanket. He hung the blue wings on his back and climbed up behind the steering wheel again.

"Hey, stay chill, Jadran," said Mika. She gave us a

bag of marshmallows for the trip. "And don't eat them all in one go!" Mom got the box of sedatives.

Jadran smiled his toothpaste smile and started the engine. The smoke made Mika cough. Mom thanked her and clambered up onto the seat opposite me.

"Are you sure about this?" asked Mika again.

We waved until the red Volvo was just a dot.

The tractor rumbled through the town. And we were attracting a lot of attention today too. Only we didn't have to hide anymore. It was actually nice when people pointed at Sprig or called after us.

Jadran sat proud and upright and he kept his tongue in his mouth. The blue wings bobbed up and down.

As soon as we were out of the town, Sprig took off. He floated along on the wind and tumbled over the meadows like a gigantic baby pigeon. My whole body was soon cramped up again and all my bones were creaking. But I didn't care. I was enjoying every second together on the tractor.

Mom and Jadran sang one song after another. And *The Blue Angel* wasn't the only musical that Jadran still knew by heart. They sang about cats, about gangs, and about orphanages, just like they used to with Dad.

And I started singing along too. I was singing made-up words to the wrong tune. But I sang at the top of my voice.

Dad hadn't been so close for a very long time.

WE DROVE ALL DAY. THE hills became steeper and there were rocks in the grass. Jadran struggled to steer the tractor safely along the winding little roads.

Mom would rather have gotten behind the wheel herself. If Jadran missed one bend, we'd go rolling down the slope. But she stayed sitting there bravely and pressed her lips tightly together. As we drove, the robotic female voice of Mom's phone told us the way.

Sprig had no problem with the bends. He flew higher and faster. Sometimes he disappeared from sight for minutes, and then reappeared in the sky as a tiny dot.

It's time, I thought. Sprig's great at flying now. He's ready to continue his journey on his own.

The air was clammy and it was raining. Mom gave us our raincoats and pulled a plastic bag over my cast.

"Let's get out of the rain, Giant!" I shouted.

Mom stopped me. "Leave him, Josh. If we need to, I'll tell him. You've looked after him for long enough."

After the hills and valleys we'd been through, endless fields stretched out into the distance. Twisting little rivers gave way to a perfectly straight canal. I wondered where that canal would flow into the sea. And if it was a good place for snorkeling. Jadran could be as jealous as he liked, but as soon as my leg had healed I was going to diving club.

We ate at a roadside diner and Jadran got to give his hands a good wash. He splashed soap all over the floor of the men's bathroom.

Mom's telephone rang twice. First Murad called, and then Mika, but Mom didn't answer.

"Not right now," she said with a smile. "Now it's up to us."

"We're nearly there," said Mom when the sun was low above the tops of the trees. Grapes were growing on the hills here, and there were half-timbered houses.

She guided us along a narrow road through some marshland. Gnarled trees grew with their roots in the water. After the marsh we came to a levee, which stretched as far as I could see on both sides.

We followed the road along the levee to a small parking lot. Jadran parked the tractor there. At the back a concrete staircase led to the top of the levee. He and Mom helped me up the steps. I put my arm around their shoulders and hopped on one leg.

In front of us was a vast lake with lots and lots of little islands. Across the water, boats gleamed in a small marina, and there was a church built on a strip of land in the water.

But there was no sign of any cranes.

"They're not here!" said Jadran, kicking a garbage can. "This isn't the south, is it? The south is in Spain. This isn't far enough!"

I leaned on Mom's shoulder and was about to start explaining and telling him that this really was the right place. That this had to be the right place. But Mom just let him do his thing. She turned around and helped me walk to a little white building with a climbing frame in front of it. A picnic table stood under a canopy, and there was a firepit.

"We'll wait here," she said. "Until the birds come."

"Are you sure they will?"

"During the daytime they look for food in the fields, but in the evening they come back to this lake to sleep. I read about it on the website."

Mom fetched our warmest clothes from the tractor. She gathered wood among the bushes and made a fire in the pit. Then she showed us how to roast marshmallows without burning them. We stabbed them onto a stick, one by one. Jadran dropped one into the fire and another one went completely black.

"These are so good!" he said. "These are the best thing ever, huh?"

Mom rubbed some white goo off his chin.

We held long sticks in the flames. With the glowing tips we drew shapes in the air: the wheels of the tractor, dancing birds, and a hang glider.

Jadran tried to write a word in crane letters.

I drew a smoking zombie town.

In the twilight the first cranes came flying over. They trumpeted loudly as if they wanted to say hello.

Krrroo krrroo krrroo!

Jadran started to jump up and down on the levee. Mom stood close to the wheelchair and put her hand on my shoulder. Sprig stretched his neck when he saw the other cranes. He opened his beak to call something back, but the high-pitched soccer referee's whistle was broken. And his squeak wasn't working very well either.

"Go on, Sprig," I said. "You can spend the winter here safely."

Jadran pulled a sad face, but he tried to encourage Sprig too.

"This is the south," he said. "Not the south in Spain, but south enough. Look, there's your family!"

Above the lake, a huge spectacle erupted. Cranes came flying from all over. They floated low before the setting sun, flew in long ribbons over the water, looking for a place to land and sleep. Groups of hundreds, maybe thousands, of birds were gathering here for the night. For some of them it was just a stop on the way to Spain or North Africa, but many of them spent the whole winter here.

Jadran spread the blue wings. He flapped and flapped, but Sprig didn't move.

"Up!" he shouted. "Up!" And he started running along the levee.

If he didn't pay attention, he might slip and fall into the water. But Mom and I didn't say anything. We both watched as he ran faster and faster, trying to tempt Sprig into flying. And it actually worked. The young crane started to follow him. He stamped his feet and did funny little hops.

And all that jumping shook his voice back into his throat.

Kri kroo-ee, he went as he hopped along. This was a new sound. *Kri krrroo kroo-ee!* It sounded almost like a little trumpet. A small, dented, and out-of-tune little trumpet, but it still blared away.

And it wasn't long before, blaring away, Sprig took off into the air.

The islands were grey with cranes. They shook out their feathers and rubbed up against one another on their long stilts. And they made such a wonderful noise that my ears were singing.

As Jadran came running toward us, Sprig suddenly swerved left. He zoomed over the reeds that grew at the edge of the levee and flew to the middle of the lake.

Jadran stopped. He cupped his hands around his mouth and shouted as loud as he could, "Sprig, wait a moment . . . Spriiiiiig!"

And Sprig answered from a thousand throats at once.

Krrroo kroo-ee krrroo krrroo kroo-ee!

"I have another beetle for you! I want to give you a hug. I . . ."

"It's okay, Giant," said Mom. "He can manage by himself from here."

Jadran closed the wings and looked at me.

"Is he coming back?"

"Maybe," I said.

"When's maybe?"

Mom took Jadran's hand and gave it a squeeze.

"You are the best daddy crane I've ever seen," she said.

For a long time, we stood watching. Pretty soon we lost sight of Sprig. The water splashed against the levee. An owl called out near the little church.

"There he is!" Jadran shouted. "No! There!"

But we couldn't see if it was really Sprig.

We didn't leave the levee until the last cranes had landed and they were all keeping their beaks shut. Jadran picked me up and carried me down the stairs to the parking lot in his arms. Surrounded by all his feathers, I felt like a little baby chick.

"We should head home," said Mom.

"Which home?" I asked.

"Our own little apartment."

"Do you think Mika will mind if Giant . . . ?"

Jadran blew his breath onto the back of my neck. "Like sparrows, that's what she said, huh? We live like sparrows, all snuggled up together."

Mom smiled cautiously. "We'll give ourselves another chance. And Mika can help us."

"Mika can do everything." Jadran chuckled. "I'm going to marry her."

At the bottom of the levee, he put me on the ground. In the darkness, the tractor looked like a big animal.

"Wanna get going then?" I said after Mom had let Murad know we were about to leave. He was going to come meet us in the car, so we didn't have to drive the tractor all the way back.

"Always, hey, little guy? Always!" Jadran answered, way too loud.

He bent his arm, pushed his head into the blue feathers, and whistled on his elbow like no one else could.

THE BLUE ANGEL

The Blue Angel is a movie by Josef von Sternberg from 1930, in which Marlene Dietrich played the starring role. The song that Jadran sings, “Falling in Love Again,” is based on the most famous song in the movie (in German, “Ich bin von Kopf bis Fuß auf Liebe eingestellt”). There are no blue wings in the movie itself, but there are blue wings in the musical adaptation by Josh and Jadran’s mom and dad.

ACKNOWLEDGMENTS

When I was small, Karel, the boy who lived next door, made quite an impression on me. He was very different from Jadran and this is definitely not his story, but my memory of him really helped me when I was writing *The Blue Wings*. Even when he was no longer living at home, Karel often used to come visit. Sometimes he slipped away from the care center and walked all the way home. One day I drove him back there myself. I'd only just gotten my driver's license and I wasn't sure of the route. But there was no way we could get lost, because Karel knew every house and every hedge.

When I was writing this book, I appreciated the support of a lot of people. My children and my wife were kind enough to go crane-watching with me for hours on end—and at an ungodly time in the morning too. We saw them on vacation in Sweden, and in the winter we went on a crane expedition to Lac du Der in France. They made the biggest impression on me when they flew, blaring away, over our own little farm in the springtime. The International Crane Foundation and the Great Crane Project gave me advice about how exactly young cranes grow up and what kind of sounds they make.

I got very valuable feedback from my sister Tine, who works as a pedagogical professional with young people who need extra care. On a daily basis, she visits schools and families and gives support to children in their unique development. Other people helped me with smaller things, like

Pierre, who taught me how to fold up his wheelchair, and Valère, who let me sit at the steering wheel of his old Fiat 450.

I'm very grateful to the fantastic team from Querido NL and particularly my editor, Belle, for her keen insight and her endless faith in me. It was wonderful to be able to work with Martijn for the interior drawings of the cranes. I'd also like to thank everyone who listened to my early ideas or who was willing to read the manuscript. Special thanks to Laura for her beautiful English translation, and to the whole team at Levine Querido for sharing my story with a new audience in the best possible way.

The Blue Wings is a book about family, friendship, and the longing for a warm home or nest. Thanks to my family, past and present, for teaching me how incredibly valuable all of that is. We're all one another's guardian angels.

SOME NOTES ON THIS BOOK'S PRODUCTION

The art for the jacket was created by Chris Sheban primarily in watercolor, with a number of layered washes to build up color and value. Once dry, Prismacolor pencil, pastel, and gouache were added over the watercolor to define lighter areas, like the clouds and the reflections on the water. The jacket art was printed on 157 gsm Oji Zunma FSC™-certified glossy art paper. The art for the interiors was created by Martijn van der Linden using tint white, carbon black, and cerulean blue acrylic paint on paper. The text was set in Sabon MT, a serif typeface designed by the German-born typographer and designer Jan Tschichold in 1964 and based on types by Claude Garamond. The display type was set in Steadfast, a full bodied sans serif font designed by Todd Masui. Initial caps and headings were set in Wicked Grit, an eroded font designed by AJ Paglia. The book was printed on 120 gsm woodfree FSC™-certified paper and bound in China.

Production was supervised by Leslie Cohen and Freesia Blizard
Book jacket and interiors designed by Sheila Smallwood
Edited by Arthur A. Levine